"You can be in the room if you
want to, Lane.

No matter what, it's your baby and I'm okay with
you being in there with me, so it's your decision.
And you know my mom and my sisters will be in
and out no matter who goes to the classes with
me."

"If I miss it, I'll always regret it. I know I will."

"Then we'll do it together."

She realized his hand was not only still covering
hers, but his fingers had slid between hers so they
were *almost* holding hands.

When he looked down, she knew he was aware of
it, too. For a long moment, there was nothing but
the fast beating of her heart and the sound of their
breaths. He slowly pulled his hand away.

Friends, she reminded herself. More than anything,
they needed to learn to be friends. She'd learned
the hard way that giving in to the heat still
simmering between them didn't get them any
closer to that goal.

Dear Reader,

Welcome back to Sutton's Place Brewery & Tavern!

Sometimes there's a trope or theme that a writer loves to explore, and reunion romances are one of mine. I love writing about two people falling in love, but when those characters have been in love before but hurt each other in the past, there are so many emotional layers to sift through.

In *Expecting Her Ex's Baby*, it has been ten years since Evie Sutton divorced Lane Thompson, and if you read the first two books in the series—*Her Hometown Man* and *An Unexpected Cowboy*—you already know they've never gotten over each other. Lane and Evie have gotten through the last decade mostly by avoiding each other, but with the brewery about to open and their close-knit family and friends holding them together, that hasn't been an option anymore. And now, well, she's expecting her ex's baby.

It was a joy to write Evie and Lane's journey as they come to terms not only with their impending parenthood, but with the emotions they've never quite put behind them. I hope you enjoy coming to Sutton's Place and visiting Evie, Lane and their friends and family. And Boomer, of course, who's a very good dog.

I love to hear from readers! You can find me on Facebook at facebook.com/shannonstacey. authorpage, or contact me directly through my website at shannonstacey.com.

Until next time, happy reading!

Shannon

Expecting Her Ex's Baby

SHANNON STACEY

HARLEQUIN
SPECIAL
EDITION

HARLEQUIN®
SPECIAL EDITION™

ISBN-13: 978-1-335-72412-0

Expecting Her Ex's Baby

Copyright © 2022 by Shannon Stacey

For questions and comments about the quality of this book, please contact us at CustomerService@Harlequin.com.

Harlequin Enterprises ULC
22 Adelaide St. West, 41st Floor
Toronto, Ontario M5H 4E3, Canada
www.Harlequin.com

Printed in U.S.A.

A *New York Times* and *USA TODAY* bestselling author of over forty romances, **Shannon Stacey** grew up in a military family and has lived in many places before landing in a small New Hampshire town where she has resided with her husband and two sons for over twenty years. Her favorite activities are reading and writing with her dogs at her side. She also loves coffee, Boston sports and watching too much TV. You can learn more about her books at www.shannonstacey.com.

Books by Shannon Stacey

Harlequin Special Edition

Sutton's Place

Her Hometown Man
An Unexpected Cowboy

Blackberry Bay

More than Neighbors
Their Christmas Baby Contract
The Home They Built

Carina Press

Boston Fire

Heat Exchange
Controlled Burn
Fully Ignited
Hot Response
Under Control
Flare Up

Visit the Author Profile page
at Harlequin.com for more titles.

For my dad. You've been gone fifteen years now, and I thought about you a lot while writing this series about three sisters who've lost their father. Like the Sutton sisters, your three girls are taking care of each other and we're doing okay.

Chapter One

Good morning, Stonefield! We're almost to the halfway point of August, but there's still plenty of summer left. Sutton's Place Brewery & Tavern wants to remind you that your favorite Sutton's suds are now available to take home with you to enjoy after a long, hot day. Stop by and pick up a growler Thursday through Sunday evenings!

—Stonefield Gazette *Facebook Page*

Flashing yellow lights turning the quiet night into the world's saddest disco did nothing to ease the nausea Evie Sutton had been battling for the past few miles.

She didn't move, willing herself to keep the misguided slice of gas station pizza down, until there was a soft knock on her window. Her Wrangler had old-fashioned cranks, which required more motion than she was in the mood for, but she slowly rolled it down when she saw a familiar face.

"You okay, Evie?"

"Hi, Vinnie." She really hoped he'd just been driving by and nobody had actually called out the tow truck to rescue her.

But she tapped the screen of her phone to see the time and realized she'd been sitting on the side of the road with the ignition off for a solid twenty minutes. Just before she crossed the town line, her fight or flight instinct had kicked in and she'd done neither. She'd simply frozen. There were houses around, though, and several still had lights on, so somebody may have seen her and assumed she was broken down.

"You okay?" he asked again.

"I'm good," she lied.

Vinnie nodded, but he didn't look convinced, not that she could blame him. Her blond hair was pulled into a messy bun on top of her head, and it hadn't traveled well. She knew she was pale, and she'd tried to use makeup to put on a brave face, but the air-conditioning in her Jeep had quit on her somewhere in Pennsylvania and it wasn't a good look.

"Whatcha doin'?" Vinnie asked, and she knew that translated to him recognizing this was weird and being unwilling to leave her on the side of the road.

"Just staring at the Welcome to Stonefield, New Hampshire sign." It was the truth, but she probably shouldn't have said it aloud, because it did nothing to convince him she was fine.

"Do you want me to call Ellen for you?"

"No!" Her mother getting a phone call at this time of night from the tow truck driver was the last thing she needed. "I appreciate you stopping, Vinnie, but I'm okay. I promise. Did somebody call you?"

"Nah. I got called out for a dead battery and was on my way home when I saw you sitting here."

Since she'd known Vinnie for most of her life, she knew he wasn't going to leave until he was convinced she wasn't stuck here, so she smiled and turned the key in the ignition. Once it was running, she gave him a smile. "I appreciate you stopping. I guess I should get home now."

Her voice cracked slightly on the word *home* and she cleared her throat. Technically, Stonefield hadn't been her home since she divorced her husband and left town ten years ago. Every visit since had been temporary, even the extended visit earlier in the year that had led to her current predicament.

He patted the top of the Jeep. "Good to see you, Evie. You drive safe."

She had no choice but to put the vehicle in gear and pull out onto the road. It was time to go home—

time to face the music. Pay the piper. Bite the bullet. Take her medicine. There were so many expressions for owning up to the consequences of one's actions, and none of them made her present situation any easier to swallow.

It was almost midnight when she pulled into her mother's driveway and killed the engine, and the huge Queen Anne home she'd grown up in was dark. So was the carriage house, which the family had converted into a brewery and tavern after her father passed away, making his long-held and heavily mortgaged dream come true.

Now that she'd arrived and there was no turning back, the nausea abated some, though she still got out of the Jeep in slow motion. After stretching her sore muscles, she grabbed her overnight bag off the passenger seat and closed the door as quietly as she could.

Then she had to stifle a scream when she turned and almost walked into Mallory. Her sister—the middle child—was in an oversize T-shirt and sleep pants, and judging by her hair, she was either a very restless sleeper or had been interrupted having a private moment with her new husband.

"Evie, what are you doing here?" Mallory pulled her into a fierce hug, overnight bag and all. "Why didn't you tell anybody you were coming?"

She wasn't ready to say what she was doing there, and she hadn't told anybody she was coming because right up until she pulled into the driveway, she hadn't been sure she wouldn't change her mind and turn around. "Are you kidding me? Back in the spring, Irish and that massive diesel truck of his backed a camper in here and nobody woke up, but I park my Jeep and two seconds later you're in the driveway?"

Mallory grinned, no doubt thinking of the day she'd woken up to find an unexpected cowboy camping in the driveway. He'd been there to visit his old friend Lane, and Mallory had ended up marrying him almost two months ago. "When you have a lot of alcohol and a reasonable amount of money on the premises, you put in cameras. I recognized the Jeep, which is why I'm out here and not Irish."

She'd barely finished speaking before Evie spotted Gwen, her oldest sister, across the street. She and Boomer—the Lab and German shepherd mix dog they all adored—walked out of the house she now lived in with Case Danforth, crossed the road and joined them in the driveway.

"Evie, what are you doing here?" She also hugged Evie and her overnight bag. "I was in my office, writing down a few notes for my book, and Boomer came and got me. I think he knows all of our vehicles just by the sound."

Evie set down the bag so she could greet Boomer with proper scratches and belly rubs, but her stomach was rolling again. It was time to confess because there was no turning back now. She stood and faced her sisters, tears gathering in her eyes.

"I'm pregnant," she said out loud for the first time. "I'm here to tell my ex-husband we're having a baby."

Lane Thompson wasn't in the mood for problems on the job today. He'd gotten up on the wrong side of the bed after yet another dream of Evie, and one of the guys calling in sick with what sounded suspiciously like a hangover hadn't cheered him up any.

Dreaming about his ex-wife was definitely harder on his frame of mind than an employee lying to get out of work. Especially the dream he'd had. The sex dreams left him frustrated, but he didn't wake feeling gutted. Last night it had been the worst kind of dream—the ones that felt less like dreams and more like memories of a marriage his subconscious was tormenting him with.

They'd been raking the yard, drawing the crisp multicolored leaves into one giant pile. Every time the breeze picked up, sweeping some of the leaves away, Evie would laugh that light, almost musical laugh he missed so much and chase after them. When they were finally finished, he wasn't surprised when she threw herself backward into the pile, arms outstretched and her laughter ringing through the neighborhood. His fun, carefree wife rarely missed an opportunity to bring herself—and the people around her—a little joy. And he didn't resist when she turned him helping her up into her pulling him down into the leaves with her.

Then his alarm went off, jerking him out of the dream that had felt so much like real life that he had a few moments of mourning the loss all over again. Those simple moments before his dad had died and everything had gone to hell—before she told him she was divorcing him and leaving Stonefield—had been sucker punching him in his dreams for years.

Lane needed Evie out of his head. Since she'd left town almost three months ago, she'd been all he thought about, no matter how hard he tried to distract himself. Their divorce years ago—when they were still barely adults—should have been the end of it. But in all of those years, he hadn't found a woman who could make him forget her. Every time she came back to visit her family, it reopened the wound loving her wouldn't let heal. When she'd come back to Stonefield to help open the brewery, she'd stayed nine months. Seeing her every day—because *he* was the brewer who'd gone into business with her father before he died unexpectedly—had been torture. Then she'd taken off *again* and it had been so much worse.

They never should have had sex back at the end of April.

That had been a hard-learned lesson. No matter how much the tension was building between you, never have sex with your ex-wife because no matter how good it was—and sex with Evie was amazing—it couldn't erase the past. Nothing could ever change the fact his life had been altered when his dad passed away and Evie hadn't liked the new version, so she'd left him.

"You planning to start that chain saw or are you trying to set that tree on fire with your eyeballs?" Case yelled to him.

Lane leaned over the edge of the bucket he was tethered into, glaring at his cousin and best friend. They owned D&T Tree Service and had run it together since they'd inherited it from their fathers, who'd started the company.

Some days, Lane wished he had a cushy office job somewhere, rather than burning himself out being a co-owner of two businesses. D&T Tree Service by day and Sutton's Place Brewery & Tavern by night. He was tired.

Once they'd limbed and dropped the very tall and very dead tree without crushing either the customer's garage or the neighbor's house, it was time for a break. The younger guys immediately went to the truck to get their cell phones in order to catch up on everything they'd missed during the brief time they'd actually worked. Lane had instituted the phones-in-the-truck rule several months ago, when one of the guys almost knocked another guy into the chipper because he was walking and texting.

Usually, he and Case would get the Thermos of coffee out and chat during the break. Case liked to use the time to talk business because Lane was a captive audience and couldn't duck the conversations. And with the brewery taking up so much of

Lane's time, they didn't have a lot of opportunities to talk about the tree service outside of on the job.

But he got the impression Case was avoiding conversation with him today. This morning, he'd claimed he was running late and met them at the job site, rather than driving to Lane's and riding with him. And he'd been overly attentive to Boomer, who really preferred to be left alone to nap in the shade. There was nothing specific Lane could put his finger on, but Case wasn't acting himself, and he finally cornered him by the truck and called him on it.

"You've been acting weird all morning, man. Something's up. You and Gwen have a fight?"

"No, nothing like that."

He wouldn't meet Lane's eyes, though, and finally the lightbulb went on. There was only one topic of conversation that would be awkward between them. "It's about Evie, isn't it?"

Case sighed, and Boomer picked his head up, looking for the reason his human didn't sound happy. "Could the dynamics of this family get any messier?"

"One, you should never ask that out loud. And two, you're my best friend."

"And your ex-wife's sister is my fiancée."

"You're also my cousin," Lane pointed out. "Family."

"But, she's almost my *wife*."

"Gwen told you not to say anything." It wasn't a question.

"There are going to be times I know something that I can't talk about."

Lane crossed his arms over his chest. "I don't like it."

"I don't, either. But I love Gwen, and I do *not* want the Sutton women mad at me."

He understood that, but he also couldn't let it go. He couldn't let *anything* go when it came to Evie. "Is she okay?"

Case shot him a look, but then he nodded. That was a relief, but there was something going on. And it was something that Case was uncomfortable keeping from Lane, which meant it could be something that could affect him. Or maybe just something Case knew would upset him.

"Is she sick?" Case shook his head. "Stranded somewhere because she refuses to let go of that old Jeep?"

"Nope."

Though he wasn't sure he wanted to know the answer, Lane braced himself and asked the most obvious question. "Is she dating somebody?"

When Case shook his head again, relief flooded through Lane, but he still scowled. What could be left? She was okay, she wasn't stranded and she didn't have a new guy in her life. What else could Case be hiding from him on Gwen's behalf?

No. There was only one possibility left, but it couldn't be. He wasn't sure he'd be able to take it.

"Is she back?" he finally asked, unable to hold the question in. "Tell me Evie didn't come home again."

"Hey, Boomer, find a stick." Case pushed away from the truck, all of his attention suddenly on his dog. "Bring it here."

Lane dropped his gaze to the toes of his work boots, shaking his head. His cousin could have saved the theatrics with his dog because, even if Lane had known what to say, he wasn't sure he could have gotten the words out.

Evie was back in Stonefield. He hadn't even gotten over her leaving the last time—or *ever*—and she had come back again. She was trying to kill him. That was the only explanation he could come up with. She was going to torment him until he couldn't take it anymore and he just spontaneously combusted.

"Case, you've gotta give me something. How long is she staying?"

"Stop asking me questions," Case said, tossing the stick for Boomer to fetch. "I'm not saying anything, and it's time to get back to work."

They had a dangerous job and Lane did his best to keep his attention on the work, but thoughts of Evie and why she'd come back so soon couldn't help creeping up on him. If she'd simply changed her mind about leaving, she probably would have made it home to see Mallory get married. To randomly show up just shy of two months after the wedding didn't make sense. He would know if there was anything going on with her mom or sisters, thanks to his daily proximity to the family.

So something must be going on with her.

But it wasn't his business and it certainly wasn't his problem. Evie had run away—again—and no matter why she'd returned, it was only a matter of time before she took off again. That was Evie.

He would avoid her. He wouldn't give the chemistry that still sparked between them the chance to overpower the hurts of the past the way it had in April. Now that Irish—an old friend from his college days who'd come to visit his brewing operation and ended up falling for Mallory—was buying into the brewery business and taking over a lot of the day-to-day, Lane didn't have to spend *all* of his free time in the cellar. Brewing beer had been a good way to fill the empty hours, but being around Evie wasn't a great idea for him.

His daily to-do list was a simple one: cut trees. Brew beer. Eat. Sleep. Repeat. There was plenty of room to add one more task.

Avoid his ex-wife.

Chapter Two

*Back-to-school shopping is in full swing, so
don't forget to make Sutton's Seconds your
first stop for barely used backpacks, school
clothes and more! And Dearborn's Market is
expecting another shipment of school supplies
this week. Remember, shop local and support
our businesses!*

—Stonefield Gazette *Facebook Page*

Evie's morning started early but slowly, after a horrible night's sleep. She wasn't actually sick, but the
low-level nausea that had become her near-constant
companion kept her moving at a tortoise's pace. She

was always ready to kick it into hare gear if the nausea leveled up, though.

She also didn't want to face her mother. She'd deliberately timed her arrival for late Sunday, after the taproom closed because it wouldn't open again until Thursday night. If she gathered enough courage to tell Lane about the baby today—which she was determined to do—they'd have a few days to get their feet under them before the brewery threw them together again.

But Sutton's Seconds—the thrift shop Ellen Sutton had inherited from her parents, renamed and still successfully ran—was closed on Mondays, which meant her mother was downstairs. And it was only a matter of time before she looked outside and saw Evie's Jeep, even though she'd tried to hide it behind her brother-in-law's truck.

Before going upstairs to crash in what had officially become the guest room after Mallory and Irish moved into the big room at the front of the house, she'd sworn her sisters to secrecy. She had to be the one to tell her mom. And she'd even made Gwen swear she wouldn't tell Case, because he was Lane's best friend. He'd know she'd come back, of course. All Case had to do was walk out his front door and he'd see the Jeep. But he couldn't know why.

She'd only made it halfway down the stairs when the smell of coffee hit her and she almost turned and fled back to the bedroom. Even though she wasn't a coffee drinker, she'd always liked the rich aroma of it, but not anymore.

But she'd been putting off facing her new reality for too long. She hadn't even come back for Mallory's wedding, though to be fair, she hadn't known her sister would be getting married a month after Evie left Stonefield. She'd gotten as far as Arizona when her sister told her she and Irish weren't waiting and would be having a private ceremony at the house. That was too long a U-turn to make. And she'd needed time to get over seeing Lane again. Considering they'd ended up in bed together, a month hadn't been nearly long enough, so she'd attended by video chat.

When she walked into the kitchen, Mallory and Gwen were sitting at the table, and her mother was leaning against the counter, her arms folded and her eyebrow raised. They'd clearly been having a serious discussion about something, and it didn't take a genius to figure out it was her.

Obviously, once Mallory's sons had left for summer camp, she'd banished her husband to the brewery—or he'd fled voluntarily—and a family meeting was now in session.

"Evie!" Her mom's expression turned to one of joy, and she enveloped her youngest daughter in a strong hug. "You're home!"

"Surprise," Evie said weakly.

Ellen snorted. "Surprise, indeed. Neither of your sisters will ever win an acting award, so I know they already knew you were home which means they probably know why, but they won't tell me."

Once her mother released her, Evie sat in an empty chair and stole a piece of toast from Mallory's plate. She had no interest in the scrambled eggs, but she needed something in her stomach.

It also gave her something to do with her hands, and to focus on while she broke the news. "You might want to sit down, Mom."

"You're worrying me, Evie."

With good cause, she thought, and once her mom was sitting, she decided the best thing to do was just say it. "I'm pregnant."

Her mom actually gasped, pressing her hand to her chest. "Pregnant? What? How far along are you? And the father is…"

"Sixteen and a half weeks." She pressed her hand to the tiny bump that was barely noticeable to the eye, but had made the baby feel real and sent her on the road east. "And it's Lane's baby, Mom."

"Oh. That's messy." Her mom made a face that let Evie know she hadn't meant to say the last part out loud, even though it was true. "How did this happen?"

Evie shoved down the impulse to make a joke about the birds and the bees, and sighed. "Remember at the end of April, when we had ladies' night in the taproom?"

Her mother's face fell. "Oh, Evie. Tell me you didn't make a drunken and misguided mistake with a man you can't spend five minutes with before you're arguing."

"No, a few days *after* the ladies' night, I made a *totally sober* and misguided mistake with a man I can't spend five minutes with before we're arguing."

"But you really made the most of those five minutes," Gwen said, and Mallory almost snorted coffee out her nose while Evie threw her toast crust at her.

"Evie! Gwen!" Ellen sighed. "We don't throw food. And Gwen…really?"

"Too soon," Mallory muttered.

But when Evie looked at Gwen, she had to put her hand to her face in an effort to hide her smile from her mom. *This* was why she'd come home. When she'd been staring at the pregnancy test in the bathroom of the fairly decent by-the-week motel she'd found, she'd never felt so alone in her life. Not just alone, but *lonely*, and no matter how annoying they were, she'd missed her sisters desperately. That loneliness had lodged in her heart and weeks later, when she felt the slight bump of her baby growing, she couldn't take it anymore.

"Does Lane know?" was her mother's next question.

Just hearing his name made Evie want to crawl back into her bed and pull the blanket over her head. "Not yet. I'm going to tell him today."

"Did you come all the way back here to tell him in person?"

Tears blurred Evie's vision, and she tried to blink them away. "I came all the way back here because I can't do this by myself. I can't have a baby off somewhere alone."

When the sobs that had been lingering under the surface finally broke free, Ellen tapped into that super strength moms got when their kids needed it and hauled Evie out of her chair and into her arms. Evie cried into her mother's neck as Ellen stroked her back, as though she was a child again.

But she wasn't a child. She was going to *have* a child, so she needed to get herself together.

"You are *never* alone, no matter where you are." Her mom kissed the top of her head. "But I'm glad you came home to us. Everything's going to be okay."

When she lifted her head, she found Mallory there, waiting to hand her some tissues. After sitting in her own chair, Evie wiped her face while her sister poured her a glass of orange juice and made her some fresh toast.

"What are you planning to do?" Gwen asked once Evie had her emotions under control and was nibbling on the toast. "I mean, we're glad to have you back on both a personal and a marketing level, but are you planning to work in the taproom? With Lane? While pregnant?"

Leave it to Gwen to get straight to the hard questions. "I didn't really think that far ahead. I figured I'd throw myself back into the marketing."

Gwen didn't need to open her mouth to make her feelings about that statement known. Her face said it all. While Evie had a knack for social media, she wasn't going to earn her keep around here by taking Instagram photos.

"I'll work," she said. "I've worked with Lane in the brewery since before we even opened the doors."

"It'll be different now," Mallory said softly. "Maybe you can work in the thrift shop with Mom more."

Evie pulled a face, which made her mom chuckle. All three of them had worked with their mom when they were younger, and Evie's feelings about being stuck in the store all day had never been a secret. "Maybe."

"Let's hold off on any more of that kind of discussion," Ellen said. "All Evie has to do right now is rest after all that driving. And she needs to tell Lane and then they'll both need to take a breath."

"It would probably be a lot easier on everybody if I rented a place," Evie said. "I don't have a lot of money, but if I could find a one-bedroom for now, Lane and I wouldn't be tripping over each other."

"No," Ellen said in her *and that's final* mom voice. "You are my daughter. This is your home. Lane owns part of the business *and* he's the brewer, but if he has a problem, he can park on the customers' side of the carriage house and use that door. No matter how messy it gets, you come first."

Evie was too choked up to speak, but she nodded, and then looked to her sisters to see if they agreed. It wasn't a matter of whether or not things would get messy. They already were. Gwen was going to marry Lane's cousin-slash-best friend. Mallory was married to Lane's friend and imminent business partner.

Honestly, when she looked at the big picture, she was the one who didn't really fit in. But she'd always felt that way to a point. She'd been a surprise baby and, while Gwen and Mallory were very close in age, she'd come along six years after Mallory and always felt left out of her sisters' shared experiences.

"Let's not borrow trouble," Mallory told her, ever the peacemaker. "Even though you and Lane have had problems over the years, he's a good guy. Once he's had time to process the news, he's going to do the right thing."

But what *was* the right thing, Evie wanted to ask. It certainly wasn't Lane putting a ring on her finger because he'd done that once and Evie had taken it off. The fact she'd regretted it from the day she'd left him didn't change the fact there was too much turbulent water flowing under that bridge for them to ever peacefully navigate a boat together.

All the talk of messy connections made Evie think of something else she needed to say, though. "Mom, you can't say anything to Laura. I have to be the one to tell Lane, and it'll be up to him to tell his mother."

It wasn't going to be easy because Laura was her mom's best friend and at some point, there was going to be a lot of excitement about the two of them sharing a grandchild. But there was no way Laura could keep that secret from her son, and it would be wrong to ask it of her.

Evie had the workday to figure out how she was going to break the news to Lane. She'd know when he was done because, even if he didn't drive straight to the brewery, Case's truck would pull into the driveway across the street. If Case was done for the day, so was Lane.

Her stomach rolled—from nerves, not the baby—and all Evie wanted to do was push the toast away and go back to bed. She could pull the covers up over her head and hide from everybody and everything. But the women sitting around her and giving her smiles meant to show their support weren't going to let her do that, so she sipped her juice and tried not to look at the clock.

The minutes would tick by anyway, turning into hours, and then she was going to have to find the words to tell Lane Thompson that their wedding vows may not have stuck, but from now on, they were going to be bound together for the rest of their lives.

Lane walked into the house wanting nothing but a shower and his bed. He wasn't even hungry, though he'd eat something because physical labor demanded fuel and he wouldn't be any good to the tree service if he didn't take care of himself. It was also his night to cook, so he couldn't let his mother go hungry.

Then he found the note from her on the counter. *I'm having dinner with the Cyrs family tonight because I ran into Molly at the market and she was buying stuff for that casserole Amanda makes that I love so much, so she invited me. It's your night to cook, anyway, so I'm sure you won't mind.*

He didn't mind at all. Grilled pork chops with mashed potatoes and some of his mom's homemade applesauce became a couple of fried bologna sandwiches with fresh tomatoes from his mom's garden.

P.S.—You didn't clean the laundry room yesterday.

That, he minded. He was thirty years old—way too old for a chore list. Yes, it was his week to clean the laundry room, but it was easier for him to do it while he was actually doing laundry, and yesterday hadn't been the day.

He'd just finished his sandwiches and was about to head upstairs to shower when he heard a vehicle pull into the driveway. It was too early to be his mother, unless something had gone wrong with the casserole and she was back, hoping for grilled pork chops.

But when he stepped to the glass panes framing the front door, he saw Evie's Jeep and every muscle in his body tensed. The familiar, low-key ache in his heart flared up as it did every time he saw her, and he would have pretended he wasn't home, but his truck and all of the tree service equipment were in the parking area. Since he only folded himself into his mom's tiny compact car when he absolutely had to, Evie would know he was home.

A decade ago, he'd married her. A year afer that, she'd left him. And about four months ago, she'd walked into this house and they'd ended up in his bed.

He couldn't let her in the house again.

Lane walked out in his stocking feet and he didn't stop on the porch and wait for her. He met her halfway up the walkway and then stopped, crossing his arms. "I heard you were back in Stonefield."

"Not many secrets in this town." Her face was uncharacteristically still, and her hands kept clenching into fists and releasing again, over and over.

"What are you doing here, Evie?" He knew the question was wrong, but he couldn't stop himself from asking it. "Why did you come back?"

Her chin lifted. "This is my home, you know. My family's here. My mother. My sisters. I was born and raised here, the same as you, so I'll come and go as I please."

"You always have." She winced, and he regretted the sharp tone, even though the words were true. "But *this* house hasn't been your home since you filed for divorce, and yet here you are on the doorstep."

"Can I come in, Lane?"

"I don't think that's a good idea." The last time he'd let her in—when she'd stopped by to pick up something for her mom—they'd ended up naked.

"Can we sit on the porch and talk, then?"

"We don't have anything to talk about. You and I aren't good for each other."

She sighed, and he couldn't help noticing that she looked a little pale. And she was tired. Not just a long-day kind of tired, but the hasn't-slept-well-for-days kind.

"Actually, we do have something to talk about," she said softly. "And you might want to sit down."

He gazed into her earnest blue eyes, looking so steadily at him, and the back of his neck started to prickle. "Evie, what's going on?"

"Since you refuse to sit down, I guess we'll just do it like this." She inhaled deeply and then let the breath out in a sharp gust. "I'm pregnant."

He should have sat down. Lane's head swam and for a moment; he thought he might actually pass out. But then he steadied himself and forced his mind to focus. "And it's mine."

"No, I showed up on *your* doorstep because I wanted you to be the first to get the link to my baby shower gift registry."

"Can you just…" He stopped and cleared his throat. "Can you not be snarky right now?"

She looked like she was about to say something cutting, but then she closed her eyes for a few seconds and sighed again. "Yes, it's your baby. Our baby."

Our baby. For only being two small words, it took his brain an awful long time to accept they did, in fact, go together in that order. *Our baby.* His and Evie's.

"We should sit down," he said, turning and walking to one of the porch rockers before he fell down.

"Told you," Evie muttered, sitting in the other rocker.

He ignored her, staring off into the distance at nothing while he did the math. It had been around four months since they'd been together, and she'd left town almost three months ago.

"Did you know when you left?" he asked, turning to face her.

"No. Maybe I should have, but it was a busy time and I had a lot going on, and it took me a while to figure it out."

To figure out she was pregnant—that she was having their baby. A child. "When is your due date?"

"In January." Her voice cracked and she had to clear her throat. He knew he should offer her a glass of water, but he was afraid if he went into the house, she'd leave. "The eighteenth."

The middle of January. In five months, he was

going to be a father. It was a lot to take in, and he leaned back against the chair, making it creak.

He hadn't given up on having kids. Even if he never found a woman who turned him inside out the way Evie did, he'd always believed he'd eventually find a woman he could love *enough*. He wanted to get married and have children and all that.

Instead, he was having a baby with the one woman he shouldn't be having a baby with.

He'd used a condom. They always had, because birth control pills had messed her up when they were young, and even if she'd found an alternative method over the years, he wasn't taking any chances. Apparently they were a statistic now.

"How the hell did this happen?" he asked, and then he winced because he hadn't meant to say it aloud.

"I don't want anything from you, Lane. You needed to know, and now you know. And I don't know what the future holds, but I'll be staying in town—with my mother and sisters—to have this baby because I don't want to do it alone. What, or even *if*, you tell people is up to you." She stood, so he stood along with her out of habit. "I think you should tell Laura you're the father because it'll be hard on our mothers if you don't, and it wouldn't be fair for my family to know and not yours."

"Of course I'm going to tell my mother." He couldn't imagine why she thought he wouldn't, unless she didn't want anybody outside her family to know it was his so it wouldn't be messy when she left again. "What about *after* the baby is born?"

"I don't know," she said, and resentment punched through his shock. Evie hadn't wanted to come back—she hadn't wanted any of this—and when she didn't want to deal with what life handed her, she ran away from it. But she couldn't run away from a baby.

He reached out to put his hand on her arm, but then stopped and let it fall without touching her. "Evie, you're not in this alone. You're acting like I don't want anything to do with the child, but I'm just trying to process this. That's all."

"You can process it however you want, but you said it yourself. We're not good for each other, and a baby won't change that. I just wanted you to know."

She was walking down the steps before her words really sank in, and she was in her Jeep before he could wrap his mind around any kind of a response.

I just wanted you to know.

And then what? She'd informed him of impending paternity and that was it? He didn't have anything else to do with her or the baby?

Hell no. If that's what Evie Sutton thought was going to happen, she was in for a big surprise.

Chapter Three

After forty years of serving our community as head (and only) librarian, Carla Denning will be retiring next spring. According to the board of selectmen, the search for her replacement will begin in the coming months. In order to entice the best candidates to apply, the selectmen will be compiling a list of things to love about Stonefield Public Library and small towns in general. Comment here or use the email form on the town website!
                    —Stonefield Gazette *Facebook Page*

Unable to sit still, and with one burning question for his best friend, that wouldn't leave him alone,

Lane grabbed his truck keys and left his house. His mom would wonder where he was when she returned from the Cyrses' and might even show up at the brewery, assuming he'd be there. She popped over sometimes and he didn't want her anywhere near the Sutton family until he talked to her, so he'd taken a minute to scrawl her a note letting her know he was out with a friend.

P.S.—I'll clean the laundry room when I do laundry.

When he pulled into Case's driveway, he very deliberately didn't look at the Sutton house across the street. Instead, he focused on the fact Case and Gwen were sitting on the front porch, with Boomer sprawled out on the floor.

He'd been hoping Gwen would be elsewhere, but he wasn't turning back now. And she must have seen the determination on his face because she stood as he reached the bottom step. "I've been putting off reading a super long email from my agent about sub rights, so I'm going to go lock myself in my office and not come out until I've read every word."

Once she'd gone inside, Case gestured toward the seat she'd just vacated. "Sit. You want something to drink?"

But Lane couldn't bring himself to sit in the chair and pretend everything was okay until he had the answer he was looking for. "Did you know? When we were together all freakin' day today, did you know?"

"What?" Case looked confused, and taken aback by his tone. "I couldn't say the words out loud because I told Gwen I wouldn't, but it's pretty obvious I knew Evie's back in town and you knew then that I knew."

"Did you know she's *pregnant*?"

Case's eyes widened and he pushed himself out of the chair. "What? Evie's pregnant?"

His cousin not only had zero acting skills, but had never lied to him a day in his life, and Lane's body went so limp with relief, he went and sat down. "Yeah."

"Who's the... How pregnant is she?"

"It's my baby."

"Oh, shit." Case scrubbed a hand over his face. "Okay, we need a drink. Stay there."

When Case went inside, Lane had nothing to look at but the house across the street, and the carriage house they'd all worked together to convert into the brewery he and David Sutton had dreamed of opening. Evie's Jeep was in the driveway, which meant she was in that house right now, just living her life while carrying his child.

Boomer stood with a sigh and rested his head on Lane's knee, dragging his attention away from the Suttons and to his big brown eyes. "Hey, Boomer. You're a good boy, you know that?"

The tail wag confirmed that Boomer did, in fact, know he was a good boy.

"I know he's your best friend," he heard Gwen saying in a voice just loud enough to be heard from Lane's spot on the porch. "She's my *sister*, Case, and I couldn't tell you until she'd told *him*."

Lane couldn't hear the response, but a couple minutes later, the door opened and Case stepped out with a glass in each hand. Lane could tell it was probably rum and Coke, and right now he was thankful for the fact Case couldn't mix a drink to save his life and that one glass would be enough to put a dent in the turmoil turning him inside out.

"Don't be mad at Gwen," he said, accepting the glass. The first sip made his eyes water, and he knew he'd come to the right place.

"I'm not mad at her. I just can't believe she didn't tell me. I mean, we're not married yet, but I'm her *guy*, you know?"

"And if they'd told you and you weren't allowed to tell me?" Lane shook his head. "If you and I had worked together all day today and you knew I'm going be a father and said nothing, that would have been a hard thing to come back from."

Case nodded, then took a sip of his drink and winced. "Why am I so bad at this?"

"I think it's pretty good myself." He took a long swallow just to prove it. "I can't believe I just said the words *I'm going to be a father* out loud."

"I can't, either. When is she due?"

"Middle of January." He caught himself staring at the Sutton house again and sighed. "Can we go sit in the backyard? Right now, it's got a better view."

"Sounds like a good plan," Case said.

When Lane woke up the next morning in the spare bedroom in his boxer briefs with intensely rude sunlight shining in his eyes and Boomer curled up on his arm, snoring, he decided it hadn't been such a good plan, after all. His head was pounding, his mouth was dry and the dog's weight was cutting off the circulation to his hand.

And he couldn't be positive in that moment, but he was fairly certain it was Tuesday, which meant he should be at work.

If there was one thing he *was* sure of, it was that he wasn't in any condition to be running a chain saw. Or getting out of bed. Calling in sick was the obvious plan. "I'm not going to work."

Being your own boss really took the work out of calling in sick, but saying the words aloud at least woke up Boomer and gave Lane the opportunity to retrieve his arm from under the dog. He closed his eyes, thinking maybe he could go back to sleep until his head felt clearer, but his brain was already engaging.

Case probably wasn't in much better shape than he was, and somebody had to run the company. Imagining the crew standing around his yard where they parked the equipment, wondering where the bosses were, finally got him to roll over and sit up on the edge of the bed. Groaning, he scrubbed his face with his hands and decided he was getting Case a book on how to mix drinks for Christmas.

When he got downstairs, Gwen was cleaning up in the kitchen, but there was no sign of Case. Maybe the lucky bastard was still asleep.

"Before he left, Case said to tell you not to bother calling in sick because he saw that coming," she said when she saw him.

"He went to work?"

"He said he was sipping his drink and you were definitely not. Do you want coffee? There's a fresh pot."

Lane did want coffee, but he didn't want to sit at the table with Evie's oldest sister while he drank it. "I should get home, but thanks. I need to..."

He let the words *tell my mom* go unspoken as the realization she might already know hit him. She and Ellen were best friends, and Laura Thompson would certainly be the first person Ellen called when she got the news she was going to be a grandmother again. Evie had said he should tell her, but that didn't mean Ellen hadn't beaten him to the punch.

"I should go," he said instead.

She nodded, and then she gave him a weak smile. "I know this is a lot, Lane. And I know we're all tangled up together, which makes it hard. Evie's my sister. But Case is your cousin and your best friend and your business partner. We're going to do our best to keep this house neutral, and no matter what, I won't come between you and Case."

"No matter what, huh?" He appreciated the sentiment, but he wasn't sure how much he trusted it. Family was family.

"I'm comfortable saying that because I've known you my whole life, and no matter how upset you might get, you're a good guy."

An hour later, freshly showered and feeling slightly more human, Lane knocked on the doorjamb of the spare bedroom they'd long ago repurposed as the D&T Tree Service office. "Hey, Mom, you got a minute?"

"Sure, honey." Laura clicked the mouse a few times and the document on the computer screen disappeared. Then she swiveled her chair to face the overstuffed armchair he sat on the edge of.

Her dark hair was pulled up into a messy bun on top of her head—and not one of the cute messy buns the younger women put effort into pulling off—but a truly messy bun, and her dark eyes were surrounded by laugh lines. She'd been barely seventeen when she married his father, already pregnant with him, and he often wondered why a beautiful, fun woman was still alone.

"You don't look good," she said, her brow furrowing. "Case told me you were sleeping off cocktails at his place and wouldn't be in today."

"*Cocktails* is one word for it, I guess."

She shook her head. "That boy made me a vodka

soda once and I almost fell out of my chair halfway through it. But it's not like you to drink too much, especially on a Monday night. What's going on?"

"Evie's back again. She got into town Sunday night."

Laura's expression shifted to the vaguely pleasant blankness his ex-wife's name usually evoked in her. He knew it was hard for her—the woman who'd taken off and broken her son's heart was her best friend's daughter. It had been a lot of years, and Evie had been gone for most of them, so most of his mom's strong feelings about her had faded away. But she wasn't a fan of the effect Evie had on Lane.

"I talked to Ellen on the phone yesterday and she didn't mention it. That's odd."

"Probably because if she told you Evie was back, you'd ask her why and…that's not her story to tell." Confusion made Laura tilt her head, and he exhaled a shaky breath. "She's pregnant."

"Oh, honey, I'm sorry. One of you was bound to move on at some point, but it still must be hard for you to hear."

"No, it's… The baby's mine, Mom."

She straightened in her chair, one eyebrow arching in that way that would have signaled he was really in for it when he was a kid. "Are you… Did you… Oh, Lane. Is that why she left?"

"She didn't know she was pregnant when she left. But she left because of me, yes."

For a long moment, the soft music she played while

she worked and the lawn mower down the street were the only sounds in the room as he watched her work through her emotions. And he could see when she'd pushed down her personal feelings about Evie and her relationship history with Lane and focused her attention on what was important.

The baby.

Her eyes softened and he stood when she got out of her chair and walked toward him. "How do you feel about having a baby?"

"I don't know yet, to be honest. She told me and then I drank *way* too much, and I had to tell you before somebody else did, of course. Now I guess it's time for me to figure it out." He managed a small smile for her. "I think I'm going to love being a dad, though."

A tear spilled onto his mom's cheek as she wrapped her arms around him. "And I'm going to love being a grandmother."

He accepted his mother's comfort as he tried to imagine what the baby would look like. Maybe a son who'd someday work alongside him and eventually take over his half of the tree service. Or maybe a daughter with pretty blue eyes, blond hair and a smile that would warm his heart.

A little girl who looked like Evie.

By Friday afternoon, Evie was tired of being a sad, anxious version of herself and she made up her mind that tonight she was going to work in the taproom.

No matter whose names were actually on the legal documents, Sutton's Place Brewery & Tavern was a family business and she wouldn't be pushed out of it. Not by Lane—if he should decide to try it—but more importantly, not by her own self. Isolating herself would only make her feel worse.

She was having a baby. She was home, with her mother and sisters around her. She'd spent the evenings hanging out with her nephews. Jack had recently turned eleven and Eli was nine and a half, and they didn't know her world had been turned upside down. To them, she was still the same fun Aunt Evie, and spending time with them made her feel more like herself.

And she missed working in the taproom. She missed the customers and seeing her dad's picture on the wall. Even though he hadn't lived to see it come true, the brewery had been his dream and she never felt closer to him than when she was living it.

They weren't open for the evening yet, so she went behind the bar and looked at the wall of glasses. Many of the regulars had their own, with their names etched under the three lupines in the Sutton's Place Brewery & Tavern logo. Hers was right where she'd left it, on the top shelf with her mom's and her sisters' glasses.

The bar and the tables scattered around the room were polished until they shone, and the popcorn maker was clean and ready to pop. Behind the glass wall, and code-locked glass door that kept customers from being able to access the stairs down to the brewing cellar, was all the historical brewing paraphernalia her dad had collected over his lifetime.

She tried not to think about the fact Lane had used her birthday as the door's access code. He'd probably meant to change it before they got close enough to opening so they'd want to know it, but he'd forgotten and they'd all been together when he'd reluctantly told them it was 0812.

Since she hadn't been tiptoeing across the floor, she wasn't surprised when she heard the heavy thud of footsteps on the stairs. The cowboy hat emerged first, and then the tall, rugged man who was now her brother-in-law smiled at her.

"Hey, Evie," he said as the glass door swung closed behind him. "I wasn't sure who was up here."

"Hey, Irish. Sorry I'm not Mallory."

"Don't be like that. It's good to have you back in the taproom." When he took off his hat, she knew she was going to get a hug, and it made her smile.

The cowboy who'd shown up unexpectedly in the spring had come a long way when it came to expressing emotions and apparently he'd added hugging to his repertoire since marrying her sister.

He was a big guy and he had to bend slightly to wrap his arms around her. His beard tickled her cheek for a moment, and a wave of affection for him washed over her. But she needed to keep in mind that he might be her brother-in-law, but he'd come to Stonefield because he was an old friend of Lane's.

"I'm sorry I missed your wedding," she said as he straightened and settled his hat back on his head.

Even though he'd moved into the house, they'd barely seen each other since Evie got home. She was spending a lot of time in her room, and usually when she did see him, Jack and Eli were nearby and this was the first time she'd been alone with him.

"We missed having you here, of course, but you were a part of the whole thing."

Case's aunt Daphne keeping her on video chat for the entire ceremony and reception had definitely been the next best thing to being there. "It was a beautiful day."

"You know, Mallory hasn't really said anything about why you came back, but I've learned a lot about family since coming here, and I want you to know that you being my sister-in-law…that means something to me, Evie." His expression had defaulted to stoic, which meant he was uncomfortable talking about a personal issue, but his eyes were warm. "I just want you to know that."

"Thank you. That means a lot."

When a car door slammed outside, Evie's first thought was that Lane had arrived early and her entire body tensed, but Irish gave her an easy smile. "That'll be Mallory. Now that the thrift shop's gone back to regular hours and I'm here, she can sneak some quiet time for herself in between leaving the store and picking up the boys."

When they first opened the brewery, Sutton's

Seconds had closed early on the days the taproom was open. There simply hadn't been enough hours in their day to do both at the same time, especially with the learning curve for running a brewery and two kids to wrangle. The cut hours had slowly been eating into the thrift store's bottom line, though. Luckily, Irish had fallen in love with Mallory and decided to stick around.

Another saving grace was Molly Cyrs, who they could all count on. While she didn't technically work for Sutton's Place, she'd been Mallory's best friend their entire lives and she was practically a fourth Sutton sister. Molly was like a ray of bright sunshine—energetic and extremely extroverted— so when she wasn't working with her parents in the funeral home her family had owned for three generations, she liked to help out in the taproom.

The Sutton's Place operation ran fairly smoothly now, and Molly was often around, so Ellen would stay at the store because Mallory was free to pick up the boys from summer camp at the end of the day. Then either Mallory or Ellen would be with the boys in the evening, depending on what was going on and whether or not Molly was free. They'd found a rhythm and it worked. And having Evie home could only help.

Mallory joined her shortly before they opened. "I'm going to get the boys soon, but I wanted to check on you first. Are you sure you're up to this?"

"I have to be," she said, remembering her determination to stop hiding. "And I want to be out here. I love this place and I love working with you."

Her sister nodded. "He's usually here by now. I wonder if he's going to show up."

He, of course, was Lane. "He'll show up. He has a job to do here, same as everybody else."

"With Irish behind the bar, he doesn't have to be upstairs, though. I know he showed up to help Irish brew on Monday, and then for cleaning Tuesday. I've seen his truck in the other lot a few times."

Evie sighed. "Do you think he's sneaking in and out because he doesn't want to see me, or because he thinks we don't want to see *him*?"

"Maybe a little of both."

Then the door opened and Evie turned, expecting to see Molly's joyful face, but it was Lane. She froze and then he saw her and he froze, and it was all kinds of awkward. Even Mallory, who had been the family mediator since Evie was old enough to get under Gwen's skin, didn't seem to know what to say.

Then he scowled and Evie's stomach knotted. She didn't want an ugly scene right before they opened and the customers realized she was back. This was supposed to be a fun night for her.

"Should you be on your feet all night?" Lane demanded in a gruff voice.

She actually laughed, partly from relief and partly because the question was ridiculous. She was barely starting to show, so it was definitely too soon for bed rest. "Even if being semi-self-employed included maternity leave, it doesn't usually start until it's actually time to have the baby."

The scowl turned from one of concern to the more familiar one of annoyance. "Just make sure you take breaks if you need to."

Mallory had slowly been backing away, and Evie turned just in time to see her disappear into the small kitchen at the end of the bar, leaving her alone with Lane.

"Evie, I…" He stopped and cleared his throat, shifting his weight from one foot to the other. "I'm sorry about the other night."

"Me, too. I know it was a shock, and I shouldn't have left like that."

His dark gaze locked with hers, and his expression softened. "I guess we need to get better at communicating. Can we sit down somewhere soon? Maybe have lunch at the diner or something, and talk? Just the two of us, away from all this."

Part of her wanted to run. It was painful enough being around Lane without it feeling like a date. But he was right. They needed to get better at communicating, and they only had a few months to do it. "Yeah, we can do that."

"Let me know when you want to do it, and I'll make it work."

"Lunch tomorrow, before the taproom opens?" she suggested, not wanting to put it off too long.

He nodded. "Case and I usually have meetings

about the tree service on Saturday mornings, and then I spend some time in the brewing room. Just let me know when you're ready to go."

There was a knock on the door's window and Evie saw one of their regular customers trying to peek through the logo she'd etched onto the glass pane. "I guess it's time to open."

The taproom kept Evie busy over the course of the night. All of the customers wanted to talk to her and whenever somebody asked her why she'd come back so soon, she just smiled and told them she'd missed them. It wasn't a lie. She *had* missed this and had only left because it was too hard to be around Lane, especially after their misguided sexual reunion.

It was still hard to be around Lane, but this time she couldn't leave. She was going to stay and they were going to work through their issues until they could be friends again because their child deserved to have parents who could be in the same room without sniping at each other.

And they were going to start by having a very-much-*not*-a-date lunch together.

Chapter Four

*If you stopped by Sutton's Place Brewery &
Tavern last night, you may have noticed Evie
Sutton is back in town and back at work! We
love seeing her smiling face brightening up
the place, so we hope she's going to stick
around this time!*

—Stonefield Gazette *Facebook Page*

Evie woke to the sounds of her nephews getting
ready to go fishing with Irish and Mallory. Their default settings were fast-forward and outside voices,
and having hardwood floors throughout the house
didn't help mute them at all.

She didn't mind the chaos, though. Her stomach

was calm, and she and Lane had worked together last night just fine. Sure, there was a little awkwardness, but they were going to have lunch today and talk things through. The hardest part of coming home again was behind her.

Or so she thought, until she turned the corner into the kitchen and found her mom and Laura Thompson sitting at the kitchen table. It wasn't the first time she'd found them sitting like that, tea going cold because they were doing more talking than drinking. They'd been good friends for years, after all. But it was the first time she'd seen her former mother-in-law since finding out she was carrying the woman's first grandchild.

"Oh," she said as they both stopped talking and turned to face her at the same time. "Good morning."

"Good morning," they said together.

"I'm just going to…" She let the words trail off and pointed to the fridge.

They didn't resume their conversation while she poured herself a glass of orange juice, which confirmed her suspicion they'd been talking about her. That's something she'd have to get used to, since there would be a *lot* of talking in town once she started showing, but right now she was still getting used to the idea of her family knowing. And Molly, of course. She'd told her sister's best friend last night and Molly had let out such a joyful shriek,

Irish thought they'd burned some nachos and set the smoke alarm off.

Evie took her time putting the cap back on the juice and opening the refrigerator door while she tried to figure out her next move. Usually she'd sit at the table with it and talk to her mom, so taking her glass and going to sit alone in the living room or her bedroom would be weird. The awkwardness of sitting down with two silent mothers might trump the weirdness, though.

When she closed the refrigerator and turned, she was thankful she'd left the full glass of juice on the counter when she put away the jug because she would have dropped it. Laura was right there, her arms open for a hug. With her heart pounding— and not only from being startled—Evie stepped into her embrace.

Laura had been kind enough to her over the years, but Evie suspected that was due to her being Ellen's best friend. When Laura was around all three of the sisters, Evie could see that she was a little warmer and more open with Gwen and Mallory. If Ellen wasn't part of the equation, Laura probably wouldn't spare the time of day for her former daughter-in-law, and Evie didn't think being accidentally pregnant with Lane's baby was going to improve his mother's opinion of her.

But maybe she'd been wrong, because Laura gave her a good squeeze before stepping back. "How are you feeling?"

"I'm okay." Laura returned to her seat, so Evie got her glass of juice and joined them. She may as well get the awkward part over with.

"Do you have a local doctor yet?" Laura asked.

"Semi-local, I guess. She's twenty minutes away and I have an appointment in a couple of weeks."

"Did you give Lane the date?" Laura scoffed, waving her hand. "Never mind doing that. You should give it to me and I'll put it on his schedule."

Evie's muscles tensed and she bought herself a few seconds to think with a long gulp of juice. There was no good way to tell Lane's mother that Evie didn't really see him accompanying her to her appointments. They didn't really have *that* kind of relationship, and she'd already asked Mallory to go with her, so she wouldn't be alone. "This is just an introduction, so I can meet her. They're going to draw blood, but there won't be any of the fun baby stuff yet."

Laura's brow furrowed. "Okay, but Lane really should have all of this information."

Evie stifled her sigh. "I'm going to keep him in the loop, of course."

That seemed to satisfy Laura, because she smiled. "I remember telling Ellen back when you two first started dating that you would give us the prettiest grandbabies in town. I didn't know we'd have to wait quite so long, though."

They all laughed, and then her mother and Laura launched into a debate over whether the need to knit baby booties and blankets outweighed being surprised by the baby's gender. They went back and forth for a few minutes while Evie drank her juice, not really paying attention.

"Lane is so practical," Laura said, and as always, hearing his name dragged Evie out of her thoughts. "He's going to want to know if the baby's a boy or girl as soon as they can find out."

Evie wanted to remind Laura that it wasn't really Lane's decision to make, but starting off this new and unexpected phase of their relationship by having an argument with his mother wasn't going to make it any easier.

Since neither of the women was actually talking to her, Evie drained her glass and stood. "I'm going to take a shower and get dressed and all that. And I need to run through the tavern's social media and respond to any comments and questions and all, so I'll probably be a while."

She managed to find enough busywork to keep her in her room until Laura was gone, and then she went back to the kitchen to make some toast to hold her over until lunch. While she ate, she jotted down some ideas for future social media campaigns. Then she made a note to see whether the navy Sutton's Place T-shirts they wore in the taproom were available in maternity styles. She wouldn't need them for a while yet, but she wanted to be prepared because the alternative would be borrowing one from Irish, which she'd swim in other than the baby bump.

While she moved around the house, she did her best to avoid looking out any windows that faced Case and Gwen's house. Saturday mornings were when Lane and Case would sit on Case's front porch and have informal meetings about D&T Tree Service. Laura had been handling the phone calls, scheduling the smaller jobs and bookkeeping since the men were children, but they handled the big stuff and all the decision-making. They used to do it on Saturday nights, but the taproom opening had forced a change in their routine.

When her phone buzzed in her pocket, she actually jumped. Laughing at herself, she pulled it out and read the words on the screen.

I'm ready when you are. We riding together or separate?

It didn't make any sense for them to take two vehicles since they were leaving from essentially the same place and both going to the diner. And it was awfully hot and humid to be driving around with busted air-conditioning. Based on their history, though, there was a good chance the conversation was going to go sideways and if it did, she really didn't want to suffer an awkwardly silent drive back to the house.

I'll meet you there.

All she got back was the thumbs-up emoji, so she grabbed her wallet and keys, and drove into town. She was tempted to stop by the thrift store and get a pep talk from Mallory, but she didn't really have time and she didn't need her mom making her emotional right before she saw Lane again.

It wasn't until she walked into the diner and saw that it was busier than she would have liked that she realized coming here had been a big mistake. In their desire to find neutral ground, away from the family, they'd chosen a place where their presence together would draw attention. It would be one thing if Mallory and Irish or Gwen and Case were with them because they all ran the brewery together, but Lane and Evie out for a meal alone? People were going to talk.

Not that it mattered. Once the baby bump outgrew being disguised with wardrobe choices, they were going to be talking anyway.

After sliding into the most private booth she could find, Evie looked up just in time to see Lane walk through the door.

The love hit her first, as it always did, like a blow that made her heart skip a beat. Then came the longing, but that was immediately chased away by a pang of loss and regret so strong it took her breath away. It was the same emotional cycle that had been tormenting her every time she set eyes on him for the last decade, and neither time nor distance had ever lessened the potency.

And maybe it was just her imagination—or wishful thinking on her part—but when he looked around the diner for her and their gazes finally met, she thought maybe he felt the same things.

Lane cursed under his breath when he made eye contact with Evie across the diner. He usually cursed, even if he did it silently, each time he saw her because even after all this time, it still hurt to see those pretty blue eyes. And the only way to push down the hurt was with anger.

Meeting her here had been a bad idea.

Not because of the curious glances of the diners who realized Lane was meeting Evie for lunch, though he wasn't thrilled about those. He'd wanted to get away from the brewery and her family, but this wasn't exactly private. Mostly he regretted because he really shouldn't have asked to meet her *anywhere* because he had no idea what to say to her.

Knowing they needed to learn to communicate for the child's sake was one thing. Actually knowing what he wanted to communicate was something else entirely.

"Hey," she said as he slid into the booth.

"Hey." Now that he was close to her, he could see the hint of color across her cheeks and neck. "You look flushed. Are you feeling okay?"

"It's warm in here and the air-conditioning in my Jeep died, so I was already hot when I got here. I feel okay, though. Just wish it was a little cooler."

He had no idea what to say next, so he pulled a menu from the holder at the end of the table, even though it hadn't changed in at least ten years. "You order yet?"

"Not yet. I haven't been here long."

Looking at the menus they'd long ago memorized and ordering lunch gave them an excuse to avoid actual conversation for a few minutes, but too soon they had their drinks—water for her and a coffee for him—and it was time to either talk or just stare at their beverages in awkward silence.

He still didn't know what to say.

"We're really crushing this communication thing," Evie said when the silence had stretched almost to the point of being unbearable. The smile she gave him was a little on the sad side, which made him feel like a jerk. He'd invited her here. He needed to make more of an effort, no matter how hard it was.

"My mom said you two had a talk this morning," he said for want of anything more profound.

"I wouldn't exactly say she and I had a talk. It was more like I was in the room while she and *my* mom talked." She swirled her straw through the ice cubes in her glass. "She did give me a hug, though, which was nice. I really want everybody to be happy about this baby."

She looked up as she said the last words, and Lane's gaze locked with hers in what felt like a challenge. "I'm happy about it, Evie."

"Are you?"

"I really am. Did it knock me for a loop? Of course. But I've always wanted kids. You know that."

One corner of her mouth lifted. "Just not with me."

"Obviously I didn't picture myself having a baby with my ex-wife who can't stand to be around me, but here we are."

Her jaw clenched and he belatedly realized he could have softened that truth a little. "Here we are."

"Evie, look…you can't be mad at me for not thinking you and I having a baby together is ideal. I'm happy about the baby, but that doesn't erase the fact you left me."

"It was ten years ago, Lane. The only way we're going to move forward together as co-parents is to put the past where it belongs. I left you ten years ago. A decade."

"You left me *twice*."

She held up her hands. "You can't be serious, Lane. Being around you was hard and then we had sex and that made it so much worse. We couldn't even speak to each other, so I left, but I don't think you can say I left *you*. There was no you and me to walk away from at that point."

"Would you have come back if you weren't pregnant?"

"No." She shook her head, as though to drive home the point that already felt like a punch to the gut. "And you're still making this about you. I came here to talk about the baby and how we're going to handle that going forward, not to rehash all the ways I did Lane Thompson wrong."

She was already sliding out of the booth. "Evie, wait."

"You can have them put my sandwich in a to-go box and leave it in the taproom's fridge for me."

The fact they were in the diner kept Lane from getting up and going after her—from yelling her name and convincing her to sit back down. They didn't need a gossip-minded audience right now. Instead he flagged down the server and told her something had come up and they'd need their order to go. He wasn't in the mood to sit and eat his lunch alone.

He spent the time between walking out of the diner and the taproom opening beating himself up for handling lunch with Evie in the worst possible way.

She was right. He was still so focused on how much it hurt every time she left that he hadn't taken a single step forward. But she was wrong about her recent departure not counting. It ripped his heart out every single time Evie left Stonefield, no matter how brief the visit was. Over the last decade, she'd blow into town for a holiday or special occasion—or her father's funeral—and then blow back out again, taking another piece of Lane's heart with her. She didn't know it, but Evie leaving was a wound that was never allowed to totally heal before it was reopened again.

Watching her with their customers didn't help any. Evie had always been the sunshine of the Sutton family—bright and shining with an effervescent personality that made everybody she met fall a little in love with her. He'd been drawn to her like a moth to a flame as a teenager, and not a day went by that it didn't tear him up inside that every time she looked at him, that light flickered and went out.

During a lull, when Irish seemed to have a handle on the customers sitting at the bar while Evie took care of the people at tables, Lane pulled out his phone and opened the Instagram app. He checked the brewery's account daily because he liked to see the photos Evie came up with. She had a creative soul and the account had built a solid following very quickly.

Then he typed her name in the search bar and tapped on her personal account. The most recent picture was a selfie of Evie wearing a pink straw hat that had a band made of artificial fruit. Her head was tilted and she was grinning—that sunny personality shining out at him—and the caption made him smile. *The things you find when your mom owns a thrift shop.*

Lane had started his account before he and David had decided to open a brewery, using a random brewing-related username. He followed a lot of beer makers in New England, but the one account he didn't follow was Evie's personal one. He'd seen every photo she posted, but he typed her username into the search bar each time so she wouldn't know he couldn't stop himself from looking at her pictures. Not that she was likely to connect the random username to him, but hitting that Follow button would have felt too much like a confession.

"I'm all for you staring at Evie's pictures all night," Irish said, making him jump, "but standing somewhere out of the way would be better."

With a guilty start, Lane exited the app, locked his screen and slid the phone back into his pocket. There was no sense in denying that's what he'd been doing. Not to Irish anyway. It hadn't been that long ago that, while alone in the cellar with his friend, Lane had verbalized the painful truth that had been haunting him for ten years.

Why, of all the women in the world, do I have to love that one?

Irish hadn't had an answer for him. There was no answer. Lane loving Evie was just the way it had always been, and it sure seemed like it was the way it always *would* be. Even her breaking his heart and leaving him when he needed her the most hadn't really put a dent in it.

Yeah, it was just the way of it, he thought. And with a baby on the way, there would never be enough time or distance between them to let him get over her—assuming it was even possible. He was doomed to spend his entire life loving the one woman he didn't want to love anymore.

Chapter Five

Notice to Stonefield residents in the area of Pine and Birch Streets: our intrepid mail carriers are bothered by neither rain nor snow, but the flock of wild turkeys in the area has taken a disliking to your mailman. After an incident yesterday during which the flock circled the mail truck while the tom chased the mailman around the Mulroney family's front yard (which was caught on their doorbell camera), the feeling is mutual. Until town officials and conservation officers can convince the flock to move on, please retrieve your mail from the post office during regular business hours.

—Stonefield Gazette *Facebook Page*

Three days of silence between Lane and Evie wasn't going to cut it, and Evie knew if she didn't want it to continue, she was probably going to have to be the one to reach out. And she would, because she was going to be friends with the father of her child, no matter how hard it was.

And, so far, it was *very* hard. Lane had skipped last night's weekly meeting. Since opening the brewery, Monday nights had become the unofficial meeting night for Sutton's Place Brewery & Tavern business. With both the taproom and the thrift shop closed, it was the best night for a family dinner and it allowed them to come together and talk about how things were going.

They usually opened with a general discussion and they all got a chance to raise any concerns. They talked about what was going right and things that could be improved. Then Mallory would give an update on the finances, since she was the one who acted as liaison with the bookkeeper.

Then it was Evie's turn. While she'd been away, she'd joined a couple of meetings via FaceTime when her temporary bartending job had permitted, but mostly she'd just sent the info to Mallory to share with the others. Since her return, she'd fallen into the old routine. She always opened with their social media numbers. Likes and comments. Engagement. If they'd been tagged or shared by any high-profile accounts. Their eyes usually glazed over by the time she was finished with that, because her numbers after Mallory's numbers made for a lot of statistics. Then she'd outline any ideas she had for future social media posts before getting to the really fun stuff—the events.

Lane and Irish would give updates on the beer, and anything special they were thinking about doing, but Lane hadn't come last night. Instead, he'd sent his regrets and a few notes with Irish. She'd been keenly aware of his empty chair the entire time, and judging by the looks that kept bouncing between the chair and her, so had everybody else.

This was exactly what she'd been worried about when she told her mom and sisters she should rent her own apartment. Her being around was driving a wedge between Lane and the rest of the family. She didn't want that, so she was going to rise above her annoyance with him and make peace for the sake of her family and their baby.

And just to prove—if only to herself—that she could be the bigger person, she was going to invite him to stay for supper after he and Irish were done with their weekly deep cleaning, and she'd make his favorite meal.

Before she could talk herself out of it, she pulled out her phone and typed out a text message to Lane.

I'm making supper for the family tonight. I'd love for you to come.

She hit Send and then winced, belatedly realizing the second line laid it on a little thick. But it was too late now, so there was nothing she could do but stare at the screen and wait for the three dots indicating he was typing to turn into his response. And she waited some more as the dots disappeared and reappeared and disappeared again. It felt like forever before one word appeared.

Why?

Evie made a disgusted sound and resisted the urge to toss her phone. All that dot drama for one three-letter word? She jabbed at the on-screen keyboard so hard with her thumbs, she almost dropped the phone on thc floor.

Because we need to get along for the sake of the baby AND the brewery. We're adults and there's no reason we can't be friendly.

After she hit Send, she watched the dots dance again and cursed herself for leaving him the opening to remind her there *was* a reason they couldn't be friends. Lane never missed an opportunity to bring up the fact she'd divorced him.

Fine.

She would have liked a little more enthusiasm, but at least he hadn't reminded her they weren't friendly because she'd left him again. And there was always the possibility the curt responses were due to his general dislike of trying to type out long text messages on the screen, and he was happy to have another chance to work on their communication.

Not likely, but it was possible.

By the time the family started appearing in the dining room, Evie was exhausted and couldn't remember why cooking supper for everybody just to extend an olive branch to Lane had seemed like a good idea. She hated cooking and she wasn't very good at it, and nobody had ever cared because her mother and Mallory were not only good cooks, but Ellen enjoyed it. Evie certainly did not.

"That smells good," Irish said when he came in through the back door, Jack and Eli on his heels as usual. She glanced over as he hung his cowboy hat on the large wooden peg mounted on the wall for just that reason, and happened to catch Eli's grimace. The kid obviously didn't agree.

"Lane isn't with you?" she asked, trying to keep her tone casual, but if she'd gone through all this trouble just to have him back out, she was going to hunt him down and force-feed him. He was eating the meatloaf, dammit.

"He's coming. He wanted to run across the street and talk to Case for a few minutes."

Evie nodded, and then turned her attention back to the gravy she was supposed to be whisking. It looked a little thin, but it was the best she could do.

And it wouldn't matter for Lane anyway, because he liked ketchup on his meatloaf. A *lot* of ketchup.

Mallory helped her carry out the serving dishes while the boys set the table, and the butterflies in Evie's stomach went hyperactive when she heard the front door close. That had to be Lane, and she wanted this dinner to be perfect. Their lunch had been a disaster, driving the wedge deeper between them rather than bringing them together. She needed to fix it and feeding him his favorite meal while making him feel like part of the family was going to be a good start.

"This looks wonderful, honey," her mother said as she took her seat.

Evie wasn't sure about that. The meatloaf looked okay, but the gravy was thin, the mashed potatoes were lumpy and she could probably knock somebody unconscious with a biscuit. "Thanks, Mom."

When Lane stepped into the dining room, she fixed a friendly smile on her face and turned to him. "I made your favorite."

His eyes widened, and then his gaze bounced to the table and back to her. "That's…great."

"Sit next to me," Jack said, and Lane gave her a wan smile before taking a seat between the two boys.

Once they were all seated, the serving dishes were passed around and Evie smiled as she watched Lane smother his meatloaf with ketchup. They were still in the early days of being newlyweds—they weren't even totally unpacked from moving into their rental yet—when she'd made it for him for the first time. She didn't really like meatloaf herself, but he'd mentioned it was his favorite of his mom's meals, so she'd asked her mom for a recipe and made it for him. After his first bite, he'd put so much ketchup on it, she wasn't sure he could taste anything else, but he'd assured her that was the way he liked it.

Ellen stifled a cough and then took a long drink, catching Evie's attention. After setting her glass down, her mother gave her a weak smile. "Didn't I give you a meatloaf recipe once? A long time ago?"

"Yes. This is your recipe."

Ellen's eyebrow arched. "You tweaked it a little?"

"No. I followed it, just the way you wrote it down. I still have the card." She hadn't made the recipe since the divorce, but she hadn't been able to bring herself to throw the recipe card away.

"Oh."

"Do you want the ketchup?" Lane asked, holding the bottle out to her mom, and something about the way he said it that made suspicion ripple through Evie's mind.

"We should have invited Case and Gwen over," Mallory said as she poured more gravy over her meatloaf. "Gwen loves meatloaf, and it's a shame she's missing this."

"Mom," Eli said, and then he jerked as though

somebody—maybe Lane—had kicked him under the table.

"You told me it was delicious," Evie said to her ex-husband, glaring at him in a way that made the accusation behind the words very plain.

The look Jack gave Lane would have made her laugh if she wasn't so mad. "You did?"

"It was a long time ago," Lane said, and it wasn't clear if he was talking to Jack or Evie.

"You told me it was delicious," she repeated, "and I made it for special occasions. I… You said it was your favorite."

He nodded slowly. "My mom's meatloaf is my favorite. But you were so proud of it, I didn't have the heart to tell you it wasn't…really amazing."

"I fed it to you the entire time we were married."

"I know."

"And I made it tonight as a peace offering—to be *nice* to you—and now my whole family knows I can't make meatloaf."

"Except Aunt Gwen and Uncle Case," Eli said earnestly, obviously trying to help. "We'll tell them it was awesome and they won't know."

"Thank you, sweetie." Evie managed a smile for her nephew.

Lane scowled. "So he lies about it and he's a sweetie, but I lie about it and I'm in trouble?"

"It's not as bad as all that," Irish said, but Evie could see that he'd smothered his meatloaf in ketchup and her brother-in-law didn't even like ketchup that much. He preferred barbecue sauce.

"It's fine," Evie said, pushing back her chair as she stood. "You can order pizza or something. I'm not hungry."

"Evie," Lane said, and he was probably going for placating, but she could hear the exasperation in the way he said her name. "It's just meatloaf. Don't be mad."

"It's not *just* meatloaf, Lane. It was…it was supposed to mean something."

She walked out of the dining room before he could respond, and she went straight to her room. Slamming her door gave her some satisfaction, even though they probably couldn't hear it from the dining room.

So much for olive branches.

"She's really refused to speak to you for four days because you didn't like her meatloaf?" Case snorted as he made a right turn onto Lane's street. They'd gone right from a job to giving an estimate, so the other guys had been done for a while. "I know the Sutton women can be stubborn, but four days is a long time."

"Well, to be fair, I've mostly stayed out of her way, so there hasn't been a lot of opportunity. And it wasn't the meatloaf so much as the fact I told her it was good."

"From what Irish told me, that was a pretty big lie."

"You could at least pretend you don't find this funny as hell. And what was I supposed to do? She'd worked so hard on it and she was so proud to have made me my favorite meal. So I lied. And then I had to keep lying."

"You're a good man." When Lane scoffed, Case laughed. "I mean it. From what I hear, you're practically a saint to claim to like her meatloaf."

"I need to make it up to her."

"It's not your fault Evie can't cook."

"No, but she wants us to get along and that's why she made it, and she ended up embarrassed because over a decade ago, I didn't have the heart to tell her she's really bad at making meatloaf."

They pulled up in front of Lane's house and Case put the truck in Park. "So what are you going to do?"

"I don't know. Do you have any ideas?"

"I wouldn't buy her a cookbook," Case said, and Lane laughed. No, that wouldn't go over well at all. "Maybe send her flowers or something."

"Maybe," Lane said, but flowers weren't really Evie's thing. She always felt sad and a little bit guilty when they inevitably died and she had to throw them away.

"Are you going to the taproom tonight?"

"I don't know. When I told Irish we'd be working late tonight, he said he had it covered, and if I don't go, it gives Evie some space."

"You said she hasn't spoken to you in four days, so maybe you don't want *too* much space."

"Yeah, I'll think about it." When Lane hit the button to release his seat belt, Boomer's head appeared between the seats as he rested his front paws on the center console. He rubbed the dog's snout and gave his ears a good scratch. "I guess I'll see you two in the morning."

His mom was just putting dinner on the table when he walked through the door, and he kissed her cheek. "Thanks for making supper tonight, Ma."

"You're welcome. And since you asked me to switch, you know you have to make it an extra night next week."

"I won't forget." He sat down and breathed in the hearty smell of the garlic bread that was his favorite part of spaghetti. When Case had told him they had an estimate to do that would make a healthy profit, but that the guy was a talker and they'd be there a while, he'd texted Laura and asked her to make dinner.

Because they shared a house and she ostensibly worked for him, she was pretty rigid about boundaries, and whether it was cleaning or cooking or working in the yard, they split the duties. And if she thought he might be trying to take advantage of the fact she worked from home, there was a penalty to pay—in this case, an extra night of cooking for him. The only time she'd given him a pass and shouldered more than her share, they'd been trying to get Sutton's Place open and they'd all been burning the candle at both ends. Once the dust settled, though, that reprieve was over.

"How are things between you and Evie?" Laura asked when he'd cleaned his plate and pushed it away.

"Quiet."

"Quiet as in peaceful or quiet as in you still haven't spoken since the meatloaf incident?"

Sometimes his mother being best friends with his ex-mother-in-law was a pain in the ass. She knew way too much about his personal life. "We haven't crossed paths a lot and when we have, it's been in the taproom with customers to keep us busy and fill the silence."

"I guess if you're not talking, at least you're not arguing." She gave him a sad smile. "Not much of a silver lining, I guess."

It was true, though. He and Evie had very few conversations that didn't end with them sniping at each other, and that had to stop. Obviously he needed to try harder. And maybe if he made more of an effort, Evie would, too.

And he was going to start tonight. Once they'd cleaned the kitchen, he told his mom he was heading to the taproom and grabbed his keys. He wracked his brain while he drove, trying to figure out exactly what he was supposed to say or do to put them back on the right track, but when he pulled into the driveway, he still had nothing.

The taproom was busy without being hectic or crowded, and he didn't see Evie as he made his way to the bar.

"I didn't think you were coming in tonight," Irish said when he spotted him.

"I wasn't planning to, but this thing between me and Evie's been bugging me." He sat on one of the stools, and it felt strange to be on the customer side. "She's not working tonight?"

"She went upstairs to look for something."

Lane frowned. They used the upstairs for storage, but it was mostly in boxes, which she shouldn't be carrying down the stairs.

"Since you're sitting over there, do you want a drink?" Irish asked, setting a coaster in front of him.

"I might, but first I'm going to check on Evie and see if she needs anything carried down."

The cowboy chuckled. "Good luck."

By the time he reached the stop of the stairs, Lane had to wipe his palms on his jeans. It was too much pressure, he thought. Even though he knew on a logical level that he was being dramatic, he couldn't help feeling as though the future emotional wellness of their child depended on them fixing their relationship. And the look Evie gave him when she saw who the footsteps on the stairs belonged to didn't help.

She was *not* happy to see him.

"I'm sorry," he said, since it seemed like a good

place to start. "I never should have pretended to like your meatloaf."

She actually chuckled, which felt like a good sign. "And I'm sorry I overreacted to it."

He let out a breath and shoved his hands in his pockets. He hadn't expected her to offer an apology of her own, so he had no idea what to say next.

"It's actually kind of sweet," she continued. "You eating gross meatloaf the whole time we were married so you wouldn't hurt my feelings, I mean."

"I wouldn't say it was gross. It was just…" He paused and then chuckled when she arched an eyebrow. "Okay, it's a little gross."

"Jack and Eli might never try meatloaf again. And the look Jack gave you when he thought you actually liked it?"

They laughed together, and it felt so good, he wished for the millionth time that things could be different between them. She was so beautiful and it had been four months since they'd been together and he wanted nothing more than to close the distance between them—to kiss her until they both forgot everything but the moment they were in.

"Maybe we should try lunch again," he suggested, hoping to keep the positivity going.

But the amusement faded from her expression and for a long time, she just looked at him. Then she slowly shook her head. "I don't know, Lane. It didn't go so well last time."

Ouch. "No, but we need to look forward, not backward."

Her bark of laughter was anything but joyful. "That's rich, coming from you."

His jaw clenched, keeping him from pointing out there was a big difference between her walking out on a lunch and her walking out of their marriage, but he didn't bother. "Do you need anything carried down?"

"No, I was just looking to see if there was anything worth photographing for a behind-the-scenes post, but there isn't."

"Okay." He turned and went back down the stairs before things could get any more tense than they were.

That's just how it was between them, he thought. One step forward and three steps back. And even though he desperately wanted to fix it—to be able to just enjoy her company and have her enjoy his—he wasn't sure how to do that.

Instead, he was going to take Irish up on the offer of a beer and stew about it for the rest of the night while trying not to watch her work.

Chapter Six

The High Street sign drama that's been raging for well over a year might be coming to an end. After various attempts to thwart repeated thefts of the sign failed, the town selectmen decided to rename the street. Suggestions for a new name were solicited and after most of them were thrown out as inappropriate (shame on some of you!), two alternatives remained. Unfortunately, the residents of the street in question disagreed and after having to respond to numerous unneighborly disputes, our police chief has declared an end to the process. "We're going to weld the High Street sign to its post in such

*a way it's never coming off. It'll be the last
thing standing in this town."*
—Stonefield Gazette *Facebook Page*

Monday night's meeting felt endless. Evie had
come up with a taproom event that had the potential
to be a lot of fun, so she was excited to get to that
part of the agenda. But Mallory had done a deep
dive on some alternative suppliers to bring operat-
ing costs down, so all she could do was wait and
try to pay attention. "What we have on the books
so far is something to celebrate the brewery's first
anniversary and a costume party for Halloween."

Gwen smirked. "I already have ideas for our costumes."

Evie rolled her eyes. "Couples' costumes, I assume."

"Of course. It's the best part of being a couple."

"Hey," Case protested. "The *best* part?"

When the laughter subsided, Evie looked at Mallory. "Do you have costumes yet, Mal?"

"Not yet. We haven't even talked about it."

She pointed her pen at her sister. "Irish can *not*
come as a cowboy. That's cheating."

Her brother-in-law pushed his cowboy hat back
on his head and frowned at her. "How is that cheating? I'll be a cowboy and she'll be my cowgirl."

"Ew. And also, no. The whole idea of a costume
is to be somebody or something you're not because
it's fun."

His scowl remained in place until Mallory put her hand on his arm. "We'll come up with something fun."

He nodded. "Jack and Eli heard this was in the works and they don't think it's fair they have to miss a Halloween party because they're not allowed in the taproom when it's open."

"And you told them you'd see what you could do, I'm sure," Mallory said, amused affection ruining the stern effect she'd been going for. The fact there was very little he wouldn't do for his stepsons was part of his charm.

"I think we can make an exception for a Halloween party," Ellen said. "I'll bring them over for popcorn and pizza, so they can show off their costumes. Just for dinner, and then back to the house."

Mallory made a face. "I should probably get to work on their costumes. Last I knew, they were into those Marvel movies and wanted to be each other's arch-nemeses so they could have epic battles the entire time. It was so much easier when they were babies and I could just shove them into buntings that looked like teddy bears or carrots and go get candy for myself."

"They made me watch one of those superhero movies," Ellen said. "And my house better not look like New York City did at the end of it. Evie, do you know what you're going to be yet?"

"I haven't really thought about it," she admitted.

"Laura and I have something fun planned, but it's a secret."

Evie kept her head bowed, doodling on her notebook so nobody could see her face. Of course everybody would be paired up. Gwen and Case. Mallory and Irish. Ellen and Laura. Even the boys would have costumes that went together. That left her and Lane as the only individual costumes and she didn't dare look up and risk meeting his gaze, because he knew it, too.

And they were definitely *not* doing a couple's costume.

"What else do we have?" Mallory asked, looking at Evie.

"We should have an open mic night for comedy," she said, and Lane was shaking his head before she got the words out, and she frowned at him. "You could hear me out first."

"I'll hear you out, but what I don't want to hear is our taproom having an open mic for anything. We're a brewery, not an event planning company."

"Yes, I know. All you really want to do is brew beer. But guess what? If you don't keep people walking through that door who are willing to pay for one beer what they could get a six-pack of the cheap stuff for at the market, you're not going to make the money you need to brew *more* beer."

"Our beer is worth what we ask for it."

She was annoyed with him for pushing back against her, but she didn't actually want to hurt him. "Yes, it is. I'm just saying, people are less likely to think about the cost of an evening if they're entertained. The beer is the foundation of the business, of course, but it also makes sense to keep offering things you can't get anywhere else without driving at least an hour round-trip."

"Put that on the *tabled for now* list," Mallory said. "We can revisit that idea after we think about it for a while."

"Fine, but I'm going to bring it up at every meeting," Evie muttered. "And maybe I'll start nagging everybody about karaoke again."

"We already said no to karaoke," Gwen reminded her. "And it was unanimous, except for you."

Evie rolled her eyes. "You can't say something's unanimous if there's an exception."

"Karaoke could be fun," Irish said, and all eyes turned to him.

Mallory patted his hand. "Says the man who's never suffered through a school chorus concert. This is a great town, but there's a reason Christmas caroling never caught on here."

"Let's get back on track?" Ellen asked, tapping her pen against her notebook. "What are we doing for Thanksgiving? We'll definitely be closed for Thursday, but wouldn't it be nice to have the whole weekend off?"

"It would," Mallory agreed.

Evie was all for weekends off, but she made a sound of disagreement. "I know Thanksgiving's all about family, but what about Black Friday? We had good numbers last year, and I was thinking we could do extended hours that night so people can come in after they get back from battling the crowds in the city."

"Extended hours?" Lane snorted. "Because we don't work enough."

She glared at him. "If I have Mallory suggest it, will you keep an open mind?"

He glared back at her. "What is that supposed to mean?"

"You're disagreeing with everything I say."

"Because I disagree with what you're saying, and it has nothing to do with who's saying it."

She doubted that, but they were on that slippery slope from bickering to something more unpleasant, and she wasn't in the mood for any of that. Especially in front of her family. Sighing, she went back to doodling on her notebook—drawing a small fist with the middle finger sticking up and then turning the notebook just a hair so it was pointed in Lane's direction.

"I've been giving it a lot of thought," Ellen said. "Thanksgiving was special to David. He always took the Friday off, too, because he said it was the perfect family time. No school. Not too hot, but not too cold yet. And we always had so many leftovers from dinner and dessert that I didn't have to be in the kitchen."

"Dad did love Thanksgiving," Gwen said, her voice soft with nostalgia.

"We did so many things outdoors with him,"

Mallory added. "It was like a last hurrah before winter set in."

"And we always had a Christmas puzzle, remember?" Evie smiled. "After all the Thanksgiving dishes were washed and put away, we'd start a new Christmas puzzle on the dining room table to kick off the holiday season."

"I'd like to make those four days family days," Ellen said. "No school. No taproom. No thrift store. No trees being cut down. And since we're closed Mondays, it'll be five days. Just five days of being together as a family."

Evie couldn't help resting her hand over the tiny baby bump. *Family.* The more Lane got on her nerves, the harder it was to remember why she'd come back to Stonefield again, but that was it. She'd come home to be with her family, whether he liked it or not.

Lane stared into his half-empty coffee mug while Ellen spoke because he wasn't sure where else to look. He could stare at the cartoon hand flipping the bird that Evie made certain was pointed in his direction, but that would just annoy him. And he didn't really want to look at anybody else because they all knew him really well and he didn't want to broadcast his thoughts right now.

Just five days of being together as a family.

For Lane, that meant five days of being alone. Five days of heightened awareness that, no matter how much they included him because of the brewery and his relationship with David, Lane wasn't a part of the Sutton family anymore.

He had the divorce decree shoved in the back of a filing cabinet to prove it.

Lane closed his eyes briefly and then took a long swig of coffee to center himself. He always felt this way when Evie was in town—pushed out because she actually *was* family. But it wasn't true that he was alone. He had his mom. Sure, she was Ellen's best friend, but if push ever came to shove, his mom was in his corner. And Case was his cousin. His best friend. And Irish had been a distant friend for years before he came to Stonefield, and now they were good friends.

Even with the beer that he brewed and that fueled Sutton's Place Brewery & Tavern taken out of the equation, it wasn't all of them on one side and him alone on the other.

He was just feeling sorry for himself because Ellen talking about family had landed a little harder since it came on the heels of being reminded he had nobody in his life to do a couple's costume with. Not that he *wanted* to do a couple's costume, but it would be nice to have the option.

Once they'd agreed to extend Thanksgiving through the weekend, they decided to call it a night. It was a relief when Evie closed her notebook on the personal message she'd doodled for him, and he knew the smartest thing he could do was get in his truck and head home.

But Evie thinking he'd deliberately shot down her ideas simply because they'd originated with her didn't sit right with him. He wasn't going to apologize for not wanting to let the good people of Stonefield run amok in their taproom with microphones, but he didn't want to leave with that hostility lingering between them, either.

As the others scattered to whatever they were doing next, Lane stepped close to Evie. "If you get me the keys to your Jeep, I'll take a look at the air-conditioning."

"Thanks, but Case said he'd see if he could fix it when he gets a chance."

Lane snorted. His cousin had a lot of useful skills, but wrenching on cars wasn't one of them. "You know Case fixes vehicles by bringing them to my place and keeping me company while I fix them, right?"

"I'll take it to the garage next week," she said.

"Have you seen the forecast? There are a lot of hot, humid days between now and next week."

"Why do you care, Lane? You don't have to fix my problems."

It was a valid question. He hadn't been Evie's go-to guy for a long time, and her mechanical issues were none of his business. "Maybe I don't *have* to, but I'm the kind of guy who helps out his friends—

and you and me, Evie—we're going to be friends again."

A hint of pink colored her cheeks. "Oh, we are?"

"We have to be."

"Right." She pressed her lips together for a few seconds and then gave a sharp nod. "For the baby."

"Yeah." *For the baby.*

He wasn't sure how they were going to become friends again, especially after their disastrous attempts so far, but he knew they had to keep trying. Maybe if he said they were going to be friends again often enough, it would just magically happen.

"I'll tell you what," Evie said, her breezy tone at odds with the flat look in her eyes. "After the baby's born, if the AC dies in my Jeep and it's hot, I'll ask you to look at it. For the baby. But I'm not your problem, Lane."

"You're not going to keep the Wrangler after the baby's born, are you? I mean, is it safe? And have you even tried to picture getting a car seat in and out of the backseat?"

The former flatness flared into anger. "The brewery meeting's over. You can leave now."

She walked away before Lane could say anything else, which was probably for the best. He thought he was alone until he turned and saw Gwen watching him.

"And they call me the stubborn one," she said.

"Did she tell you how lunch went?"

"No, because I was working until right before

the meeting, but she told Mallory and Mallory told me. You guys have a lot of history, Lane. It's just going to take some time."

He appreciated how neutral she looked and sounded. It couldn't be easy for her family. "The divorce was ten years ago, so you can see how little time is helping."

"Well, she *is* pregnant," she pointed out, and he chuckled. "But seriously, the two of you have never *had* to work things out. Now you have a reason to, but you can't expect to erase ten years of feeling a certain way with one lunch."

The truth of her words sank in, fanning the little light of hope that never stopped flickering. "You're a wise woman, Gwen."

"Of course I am. I'm the oldest." She grinned. "I'm wise and I also never get stuck sitting in the backseat."

After glancing over his shoulder to ensure they were still alone, he swallowed his pride. "Do you have any sage advice for me?"

Her expression grew serious and she took a few steps closer so she could lower her voice. "You guys have been a roller coaster. You hooked up, obviously. And then things reached a breaking point— again—and she left. You'd both barely come to terms with that when she's suddenly back and *bam*, there's a baby. You both need to level out."

He wasn't sure leveling out was possible when it came to his feelings for Evie. "What do you mean?"

"You're both feeling this huge pressure to be okay for the baby, but you have months to work on that. Right now, you both need to settle down and come to terms with some pretty major changes instead of trying to force a relationship bond neither of you are ready for. Just...relax."

He almost laughed out loud. *Relax?* He hadn't been relaxed since he found out Evie was back in town. But he also knew Gwen wasn't wrong. "We're both trying too hard."

She shrugged. "I think so. I mean, you've each had your worlds rocked on an individual level, so take a break on the whole *we have to come together* thing. Once you've both found your footing, *then* you figure your stuff out."

Nodding, he shoved his hands into his pockets and rocked back on his heels. "I think you're right. We do need some space and time to process everything."

"I would hug you," she said in a whisper, leaning forward, "but I think Evie's coming back."

"And that's my cue to leave." He pulled his keys out of his pocket. "Thanks for sharing your wisdom. I'll be in the cellar some, though I'll probably lie low for the most part, but I'll see you around."

"Don't forget my door's always open to you."

She said that in a hurried whisper and kept glancing over his shoulder as if expecting Evie to burst in and find her sister being friendly with the enemy, so he nodded and left without looking back.

Lane thought about what Gwen had said while he drove home. Her advice had been sound and he knew she only wanted what was best for them. If the day ever came when his and Evie's best interests weren't aligned, she'd have to side with her sister, of course, but for now it felt good to have Gwen care about him.

So he'd back off. He'd focus less on Evie and more on the fact that, come January, he was going to be a father. And as he pulled into his driveway, Lane was smiling.

Chapter Seven

While many of you will be celebrating Labor Day with a long holiday weekend, the Stonefield Police Department would like to remind you that they don't take any days off, so celebrate responsibly! And the fire department has been issuing this annual reminder since the Labor Day 2001 fire at the Patton home: even if it rains, as it often does in September, do not use your barbecue grill inside the garage.

Labor Day weekend also means yard sales! Be prepared for traffic, such as it is, to brake abruptly for bargains. We heard at the diner that Ed Daniels has spent too much time fishing this summer and has had to rescue his

gear from his wife's yard sale pile three times.
Karen is nothing if not persistent, though, so
Ed would take it as a personal kindness if
you don't buy any fishing gear you see at the
Daniels' house.
                    —Stonefield Gazette *Facebook Page*

By the time Labor Day weekend rolled around, Evie and Lane had fallen into the routine that had gotten them through the initial months of working together opening the brewery.

They mostly avoided being around each other as much as possible and barely spoke to each other when it wasn't. An entire week of essentially orbiting around the brewery and the Sutton family without actually colliding.

There would probably be some colliding with Lane at the barbecue, though, and not the sexy kind. Evie snorted as she pulled her hair through the elastic to secure her ponytail. The last thing she needed was another sexy collision with Lane. It was bad enough she'd dreamed about him last night. Again.

There was no question he couldn't be excluded from the Labor Day barbecue. Besides the business partnership, he was practically family. And during the years Evie had been away—before the dream of the brewery became a reality—Lane and her dad had grown very close. Close enough to not only gamble everything on opening the brewery, but they were willing to hide their partnership from

Evie. She hadn't found out who her dad's businesses partner was until after he passed away. Throw in Ellen and Laura being best friends, and his cousin being Evie's brother-in-law, and *part of the family* wasn't really an exaggeration.

So they'd eat some burgers together. It wouldn't be the first time, and it certainly wouldn't be the last. And there would be plenty of people to talk to, so they could continue avoiding any conversation not related to customer orders. Worst-case scenario, she could volunteer herself for a cornhole tournament with her nephews.

She was going to keep following the advice Gwen had given her a week ago—relax and stop trying to force things with Lane. Gwen had confessed she'd given the same advice to Lane, and as much as Evie hated when her oldest sister was right, it seemed to be working. She and Lane definitely weren't friends yet, but with the pressure off, they were able to be around each other without feeling the need to talk to each other.

By the time she joined the party, everybody had arrived. They'd made the side dishes and arranged some snack trays yesterday, as well as making extra lemonade and iced tea, so until it was time to put the burgers and dogs on the grill, there wasn't a lot to do besides relax and enjoy each other's company.

Everybody was scattered around the yard, but Evie took a moment to greet Boomer. Case's dog was one of the best things about being back in

Stonefield, as far as Evie was concerned. She'd always wanted one of her own, but she moved around too much, and dogs made finding a rental or roommate situation a lot more difficult. And she certainly wasn't going to introduce a pet into her life with a baby on the way, assuming her mother could even be talked into it.

As she rubbed Boomer's belly, Evie tried to scope out where in the yard she wanted to go next. Her mom and Laura were sitting in the gazebo, looking deep in one of their rapid-fire conversations. Mallory and Gwen were crouched in front of one of the garden beds, and Gwen had weeds in her hand. The three men were sitting in camp chairs near the grill, and she'd bet anything they were talking about beer or trees. She wasn't all that interested in either—or in pulling weeds—which left Jack and Eli.

They'd told Jack and Eli about Evie's pregnancy several days ago, after Ellen let a comment about the baby slip out and Jack caught it. The conversation had gotten a little awkward when Eli asked if the baby would have a daddy, and after a long silence and some panicky glances between Evie, Mallory and Ellen, Evie had told them Lane was the baby's daddy, and that they were friends and wanted to have a baby together. That was happy news for them, though Jack did look a little confused at first. Then Mallory said they could have bonus video game time and that ended their interest in their cousin.

Her nephews were in the process of setting up the cornhole boards, and they each held an end of the rope that Case had measured out for them. They played it so often, Evie was sure they could gauge the distance between the boards by sight, but they always used the rope to keep it fair.

"Are you going to play, Aunt Evie?" Eli asked when she joined them.

"Maybe later." She wasn't very good at tossing the beanbags into the holes in the centers of the boards, so playing was usually a last-ditch effort to stave off extreme boredom.

"You can be on Eli's team," Jack told her, trying to make it sound like an exciting prospect for her, rather than an effort to keep from being partnered with her himself. Eli was laid-back, like his mother, but Jack shared Gwen's competitive streak.

"Are you excited to go back to school tomorrow?" she asked Jack.

"Nope."

"How come?" He shrugged and, even though she waited, he had nothing to add. "You're starting sixth grade, right?"

"Yup."

Evie frowned, trying to figure out what had happened to her usually chatty nephew. He was eleven, so he shouldn't be giving off teen attitude vibes quite yet. "I think sixth grade is pretty fun. You're old enough to do cool stuff, but you don't have to deal with high school yet."

"Corey and me have different classes," he said, and the way he said it gave Evie the clue she needed. He was sulking because he and his best friend didn't have the same schedule.

"I'm going into fourth grade," Eli told her. "I'm excited about school, but I don't like homework."

"Nobody does," she said, ruffling his hair. "Except your aunt Gwen. I think she secretly liked homework."

"I don't know why I have to go to school," Jack said, clearly ready to air grievances. "I'm not even going to college."

Evie doubted Jack had run that plan by Mallory yet. "What are you going to do, then?"

"I'm going to work with Uncle Case and Uncle Lane as soon as I'm old enough and be the boss of it someday."

She chuckled. "You know both of your uncles have college degrees, right?"

He frowned. "They do? But they cut down trees. Why did they go to college just to cut down trees?"

Jack didn't need to know that Lane's father dying was the reason he cut down trees for a living. He'd wanted to work in conservation in some way, and he and Evie had decided they'd figure it out after they settled on what part of the country they'd like to try living in. Then the decision had been taken out of their hands in the worst possible way.

"They don't just cut down trees," she told him. "They own a business that employs people. Uncle

Case has a degree in business administration, and Uncle Lane went to Montana and got a degree in forestry."

She could still remember how desperately she'd missed him while he'd been in Montana. It had been cheaper to go there than to get the same degree in New England, but not enough so they could afford for Evie to join him there. She'd had a calendar on which she'd counted down the days until he could come home for a break. And finally, to when he could come home to stay and they could get married.

"Do you think they'll make me go to college to work with them?" Jack asked.

"I don't know." Evie was rarely the person in the family who anybody went to for advice, and having it be Mallory's kid doing the asking really brought the added pressure. "I think you don't really have to figure it out until high school, but you should do the best you can in school now, just in case. Then, when you're like fifteen, you can talk to Uncle Lane and Uncle Case."

He nodded, smiling a little. "Okay."

With that crisis averted, she looked at Eli, who gave her a gap-toothed grin. "I'm going to make beer with Irish."

Evie was pretty sure that, no matter what Irish did, that's what Eli would want to be when he grew up. He absolutely adored his new stepfather. "Probably not until you're old enough to drink it, though."

Jack laughed. "It would be funny if they let him make beer and it was really gross because he can't taste it to see if it's good."

She laughed with the boys, because it *would* be funny, as long as she didn't have to serve it to their customers. And maybe it was the nostalgia that had swept over her when she'd thought about missing Lane while he was in Montana, but when she caught Lane watching them laugh, she didn't turn away. Instead, she watched as he smiled and started toward them while the other two guys began fiddling with the gas grill.

"Look!" Eli said, grabbing his brother's arm. "Mom went in the house and Irish is playing with Boomer. Let's go talk about dogs with him."

"Mom doesn't think it makes sense to get a dog at the beginning of the school year," Jack explained as Lane reached them. "But we really want one and so does Irish, so we keep talking to him when Mom's not around."

As soon as they were gone, Lane shook his head. "It sure didn't take them very long to figure out how that works."

Evie wondered if their child would do that— play them against each other in an effort to get what the child wanted. There was no doubt, she thought. Whether their parents were married or not, it seemed to be one of the primary tools in every child's parental manipulation toolbox. "Did you know Jack's goal in life is to take over the tree service?"

Lane chuckled. "Is he going to wait until Case and I retire, or should we be preparing for a hostile takeover situation?"

"You never know with that one."

They laughed together, and then Evie heard Mallory calling her to help carry out the food. The timing was perfect—she smiled at Lane and then walked away wrapped in a bubble of positivity. That was the key, she thought. When she ended up close to Lane, they could joke around and keep it light, but then separate before the conversation turned to anything serious and the sniping at each other began.

And, dammit, Gwen had definitely been right.

The first anniversary of Sutton's Place Brewery & Tavern opening its doors was a success, Lane thought as he looked out over the full taproom. Everybody was having a good time, and they were enjoying the pumpkin spice beer he and Irish had somewhat reluctantly concocted. It was too sweet for their taste and the orange-tinted sugar crystals they were rimming the glasses with were making everything sticky, but the customers liked it.

As much as he enjoyed working with Irish behind the bar, Lane had felt more than one pang of regret and sorrow over the course of the night. David should have been beside him. It was their dream together, and it wasn't fair that his friend hadn't lived to see it come true.

He knew Ellen was feeling his loss extra keenly tonight, too. She'd visited the taproom earlier in the evening, greeting people and making small talk, but he'd been able to see how hard she was working to hold it together.

David's daughters also felt it. Gwen didn't always cross the street to the taproom, but she'd made sure she was there at the same time as her mother, offering emotional support. Mallory had gravitated toward Irish a little more than she usually did, getting comforting words and touches from her husband.

But Evie probably had it the hardest, because she interacted with everybody who walked through the door, and most of those people knew the significance of the day and wanted to talk about David.

"You doing okay?" he asked when she leaned on the bar to wait for Irish to fill an order.

"Yeah." She smiled, though there was a hint of sadness in her eyes. "I'm focusing on how happy Dad would have been tonight. He would have loved this and he wouldn't want us to be sad, so I'm just accepting all the love and celebration for him and tucking it away in my heart."

Trust Evie to see the brighter side of things. "If you need a break, just let me know and I'll take over."

He braced himself for her response because she'd probably snap at him that she was capable of tak-

ing care of herself or that he was being overpro-
tective because of the baby, but she just smiled at
him again. "Thanks. I will, but I really am okay."

Buoyed by another interaction between them that
didn't go south, Lane refilled a few glasses and
wiped yet more sugar off the bar. He was glad the
pumpkin spice was a *very* limited brew, no matter
how popular it was.

Irish poured more sugar crystals into the small
plate they were using so they'd be ready for the next
glass. "I've fielded more requests for the hard stuff
tonight. A lot of guys like a shot of whiskey to go
with their beer."

Lane shook his head. "With the license for beer
and wine, we're good. But if we want a full liquor
license, we'll have to expand the menu and kitchen
and stop allowing customers to get deliveries from
Stonefield House of Pizza because to get the full
license, half of our income has to come from food
every year."

Irish shook his head. "Some of the rules in this
state are ridiculous."

"Yup. David and I talked about it before he
passed away, but we decided against it because
going into the hard liquor business actually means
going into the restaurant business, and that was
more than either of us wanted to take on. We just
wanted to brew beer." He glanced down the bar to
make sure nobody was trying to get his attention.
"Honestly, I've played with some numbers for build-

ing on to the carriage house to expand the kitchen, but it won't work."

"It would cut into the parking, for one thing. And you'd not only have to upgrade all the equipment, but you'd have to hire a full kitchen staff."

"We," Lane reminded him. "*We* would have to do all that. I think it could work with some careful planning and more debt, but if I made a pros-and-cons list, the biggest con is the increase in the level of intoxication. We're in Ellen's backyard, and there are the kids to consider. Staying beer only—especially at the prices we charge—makes it a lot more unlikely anybody's going to go staggering around the yard."

"That's a valid point." Irish nodded. "I like it the way it is."

Mallory, who'd taken a break to have dinner with her kids, walked in with two small pieces of poster board in her hand. She walked straight to the bar and set them down in front of Lane and Irish.

Closed Sunday the 18th. Going apple picking!

"Mom wants you to hang one over the bar and one on the door to let people know we'll be closed next Sunday," she said. "And before either of you make the argument you can stay open with a smaller staff, she said this will be a family trip and she doesn't want to hear it."

She was looking at Irish when she said it, so Lane stepped slightly sideways, as though to remove himself from the conversation. They could do their family trip to the orchard and he'd just have a Sunday off to do whatever he wanted. Apple picking wasn't really his thing.

"I don't remember this coming up at the last meeting," Irish said.

Mallory shrugged. "She probably didn't want to give everybody a chance to say no."

Lane wanted to point out that Ellen really shouldn't be able to declare the taproom closed whenever it suited her, but he kept his mouth shut. They'd already vetoed her desire to be closed *every* Sunday, because they made too much to not be open that day. And for Lane, it was a business, but for the Suttons—especially Ellen—it was a *family* business, and there was no sense in working as hard as they did if the family aspect fell by the wayside.

"Are you going?" Mallory asked, and Lane realized she was talking to him.

"I don't think so."

"It'll be fun."

He chuckled. "Sure, if you like apple picking."

"You sure don't mind the apple pies, though." She winked at him and headed toward the kitchen.

"Mallory." He called her back and then wished he hadn't. But it was too late, because she was looking at him expectantly. "I, um… I don't think Evie should be climbing ladders. Or carrying too much. Maybe she should only fill her bags halfway."

He didn't like the gleam in her eye, but she smiled and nodded. "We'll take care of her."

A few minutes after her sister disappeared into the kitchen, Evie stepped up to the bar with a customer order. Then she saw the sign. "Oh no. Apple picking? Really?"

Lane tapped the sign. "According to Mallory, it's not optional, either. Ellen said she doesn't want to hear it. Luckily, it's a Sutton family trip, so I'm exempt."

She narrowed her eyes at him. "You know Laura's going to go, which makes it a Sutton-Thompson family trip, from which you are *not* exempt."

"Yeah, I'm not going."

"I'm going to tell my mom not to let you have any apple pie."

He shrugged. "My mom's pies are better than your mom's pies."

She gasped, and then took the two glasses Irish set in front of her. "I'm telling her you said that."

"Don't you dare. I was kidding." Evie just shook her head and turned away. "You know I was kidding!"

Her laughter trailed behind her as she went to deliver the beer to the customers, and Lane couldn't stop himself from grinning, even though Irish was watching him. Laughing with Evie felt so good, and he'd noticed he didn't get that anxious knot in his stomach when he saw her approaching anymore.

He was definitely going to have to thank Gwen. She'd been right.

Chapter Eight

It's going to be a beautiful weekend for apple picking at the Caveney Farms Orchard! We've heard from Shawn Welch that his mother broke her leg (rumor has it a cat and a staircase were involved, though we haven't reached out to the cat for comment) and Mrs. Welch is sad to be missing out on apple picking this year, so if you go and you're feeling neighborly, a bag left on her porch might lift her spirits!

And just a reminder that Sutton's Place Brewery & Tavern will be closed on Sunday so the Sutton family can enjoy a day of apple picking, too!

—Stonefield Gazette *Facebook Page*

Getting everybody into vehicles and headed to the orchard made Evie want to run to the taproom and chug some beer straight from the tap. Of course she wouldn't even if she wasn't pregnant, but at least the visual cheered her up for a minute.

Gwen sprinted past her. "Shotgun!"

"That's not fair," Evie yelled after her. "I can't run right now."

"You can totally run. You're barely even showing. Besides, I get shotgun because I'm the oldest."

"You know I get carsick in the backseat."

"Girls." Ellen sighed, shaking her head. "I've been listening to this argument for how many decades now?"

"I hate to be the voice of reason here," Mallory said, and they all chuckled because she *lived* to be the voice of reason, "but you're having this fight out of habit. Evie's getting shotgun."

"But—" Gwen stopped, frowning. "Oh, wait. I'm riding with Case."

Ellen pointed at Gwen and then waved the finger between her and Evie. "I've always said you two fight just to fight. Obviously, I'm right."

"Old habits and all that," Gwen said. "Sure, you can have shotgun with Mom, Evie."

Evie rolled her eyes. "Thanks, sis."

They drove to Caveney Farms in a caravan, with Ellen and Evie in front, followed by Case and Gwen—sadly without Boomer because they didn't allow dogs—and then Irish's truck with him, Mallory and the boys. Laura was meeting them there, and judging by how long it had taken the Suttons to get out of the house, she'd probably have time for a quick nap in her car.

Once they'd found a place to park and gathered at the little shop that marked the entrance to the orchard, Evie had to admit it was a beautiful day to be outside, though. The air was crisp and clean, and she drew in a long deep breath.

Then a couple caught her eye and the air left her in a sudden whoosh. A mom and a dad, with a toddler between them. They were each holding one of her hands, and every time the little girl tried to lift her feet so they would swing her, they'd laugh.

It was hard to believe she was going to have a little one of her own, and she cupped her hand over the bump that was definitely a bump now. None of the taproom's customers had said anything yet, maybe thanks to the slightly oversize T-shirt she'd been wearing untucked, but the speculative looks had started. It was only a matter of time before the pregnancy was common knowledge around town, and then the talk about her and Lane would start.

"You okay?" her mom asked, and Evie realized with a start that she was still staring at the happy couple and their little girl.

"Yeah," she replied with a little laugh. "Just enjoying this beautiful weather."

"You didn't *look* like you were enjoying it. Unlike Gwen, your resting face is usually a happy one."

"Hey." Gwen frowned, then gave a little shrug. "Okay, that's fair."

The horse-drawn wagon lined with hay bales to sit on pulled up, and her mother was distracted from Evie's facial expressions by doing a quick head count. "Okay, everybody's here. Let's go pick some apples."

Just the thought of squeezing into that wagon and enduring the ride out to the picking area turned Evie's stomach and she backed away, shaking her head. "I think I'll walk."

"It's a long walk," Mallory said, while Irish helped Ellen and then Laura into the back of the wagon.

"It *is* a long walk," Gwen echoed, just in case she didn't believe Mallory.

"It's not *that* long. And I like walking."

"I can stay with you," Mallory offered. "We can walk together."

"And miss Irish's first apple picking?" She laughed. "I have my cell phone. I'll be fine, and I'll probably look around the store for a little while first, so don't try to time me and then panic if I'm five minutes longer than you think I should be. If I need you, I'll call."

"We could all walk if you want," her mom called down from the wagon.

"Ellen, she said she was fine," Laura said in a

firm voice that got under Evie's skin. She couldn't really have made it more clear she didn't want to walk with her former daughter-in-law.

"Just go," Evie said. "Don't make me slap the horse's butt."

"Please don't touch the horse, ma'am," the young man driving the wagon said in a bored voice.

Once Mallory and Gwen were finally perched on hay bales and the wagon slowly rolled away, Evie headed to the little orchard store. She loved shops with fun little knickknacks and themed gifts. Because she'd always moved around so much, she didn't accumulate many things because accumulating things meant packing and moving them, but she still loved to look at them.

The theme in this store was apples, of course. There were candles and potholders and ceramic salt-and-pepper shakers. Hand towels. Baskets. Hand soaps. The number of things that could smell, taste or be decorated with apples truly boggled the mind.

A woman reached across her to pick up a birch bark basket decorated with tiny painted apples, leaving behind a wake of perfume that made Evie's stomach do a perilous roll.

Oh no. Please not now.

She turned, desperately needing to get some fresh air, and almost walked into a person who'd been in conversation behind her. She stumbled slightly as she tried to avoid him; there was nothing she could do to avoid the hands that gripped her upper arms to steady her, and looking up into his face did nothing to calm her stomach.

What was Lane doing here?

Lane didn't let go of Evie's arms until he was sure she was steady on her feet, even though she was glaring at him as though trying to set him on fire with her eyeballs. Considering the number of hay bales and straw decorations around them, he really hoped it didn't work this time.

"What are you doing here?" she demanded in a low voice, as if she'd just discovered him in her bedroom closet instead of a very public place.

"It's an apple orchard."

"You said you weren't coming today. You don't even like apples."

He shrugged. "I like stuff made from apples, though. Apple pie. Applesauce. Apple butter. Apple jelly. Cinnamon apple pancakes."

She rolled her eyes in typical Evie fashion and pushed past him. He would have let her go, but she'd been really pale when she first turned around and he was worried, so he followed her outside. "Oh, apple crisp. I can't forget apple crisp with vanilla ice cream on top."

"Stop!" she said, loudly enough to attract attention before dropping onto one of the wooden benches. "Stop talking about food."

That explained the paleness, he thought, sitting

next to her. She probably didn't want his company, but he didn't see Ellen or her sisters and there was no way he was leaving her alone if she was going to be sick. They weren't married anymore and maybe she didn't want him around right now, but he was the father of that child, so he'd be there to hold her hair back if she needed him.

"Do you want me to go buy you some crackers?" he asked after a few moments of listening to her breathing.

"I don't think they sell crackers in there."

"I have a truck and the store's not far. It wouldn't take me long."

She turned her head to look at him, and he was relieved to see some of the color was returning to her face. She even gave him a little bit of a smile. "You're going to drive all the way to town and back to bring me crackers?"

He shrugged again. "If that's what you need to feel better."

She took a deep breath and shook her head. "Thank you, but I'm feeling better already. One of the women in there apparently got up this morning and decided to drench herself in perfume and there were too many people in there. I just needed some air, I think."

"Good." This was the part where he should get up and walk away, but he still wasn't comfortable leaving her alone. "Where's everybody else?"

"They took the hay ride out to the picking area.

I was going to go with them, but…" She waved a hand over her stomach.

"How long is the sickness part supposed to last?" he asked, realizing in this moment just how little he knew about pregnancy. He needed to remedy that as soon as possible. "Doesn't it go away at some point?"

"Sometimes it goes away and sometimes it doesn't. It's different for every woman." Her hand rubbed small circles over the little baby bump, and he couldn't help staring at it. "At least I'm rarely *actually* sick. Mostly I just feel nauseated a lot, but I was afraid that wagon ride might be too much, so I'll walk out and meet them."

"I'll walk out with you."

"Lane, I'm fine."

"You have more color now, but it's a long walk."

She chuckled. "So I've been told already, by my sisters, despite the fact we've been picking apples here our entire lives. I know it's a long walk."

When she pushed herself to her feet, he stood as well, because he wasn't kidding. There was no way he was going to sit on this bench and imagine her passed out in a row of trees somewhere.

"You don't have to go with me," she said again. "And you never told me why you're here."

"My mom called me because—"

"Wait. Your mom knew you'd be coming?"

"Yeah. Why?"

"No reason," she said, but she smiled slightly. "So why did she call you?"

"She realized she forgot her wallet, so I'm here to pay for her apples because it's not like she can put them back."

Evie laughed. "Did she think *my* mom would just drive off and leave her here with a basket of apples she can't pay for?"

"She hates borrowing money, but more than that, I think this was her sneaky way of getting me here. I mean, not the forgetting her wallet part, but realizing letting Ellen pay wouldn't give her an excuse to call me out here. She's been trying to get me to go apple picking for years. Good for the soul or something like that."

"Good for the soul?" She snorted. "Or maybe she knows she can get more apples if she has her son on hand to carry them for her."

They laughed together as they walked toward the orchards, and Lane wondered if they'd make it all the way out to the picking area before she realized he'd ignored her insistence she would be fine alone. But she seemed content to have him at her side, and he was careful to keep his stride short so she could walk at a slower pace.

She took pictures with her phone as they walked, and he wanted to ask her about some of the pictures she'd posted to her Instagram feed. But then she'd know he looked at it, of course. While she did the social media for the brewery, she kept that separate from her personal account, so he wouldn't have any other excuse than his inability to stop thinking about her and wondering what she was doing at any given moment.

So he kept his mouth shut and watched her looking for things to take pictures of. Photo-ready scenery wasn't hard to find in New England in autumn and she stopped walking so many times, he was starting to think the others would be on their way back by the time he and Evie reached the picking area.

Not that he minded. He may have grumbled when he got the call from his mom and said a few choice words on the drive over, but now that he was here with Evie, there was nowhere else he'd rather be. He couldn't remember the last time he'd simply enjoyed a day like this. If he was brutally honest, it was probably over eleven years ago, before his dad died and everything went to hell.

Then she turned in profile to him and lifted her arms to get just the right angle of a tree. Her light sweater shifted, hugging the curve of her stomach, and Lane wasn't sure if his heartbeat stopped or sped up, but it felt like an explosion of emotion in his chest and he couldn't breathe. He walked slowly forward, unable to take his eyes off the curve of his child.

"Lane, what's— Oh." He heard her inhale deeply. "I've been kind of disguising the bump with clothing choices, but it's a little beyond that now. And I guess instead of spreading out a little, this baby's just going to stick out like a basketball."

"Can I…" He stopped because he had no right to ask to put his hands on her body. "Sorry."

"Do you want to touch it?" His gaze lifted to her face, and she smiled. "You probably won't feel the baby move. I've felt some fluttering and moving, but not kicking so other people can feel it yet. But you can feel if you want."

He leaned in from an angle, so her shoulder and the side of her arm almost rested against his chest, and slid his arm under hers. Tentatively, he brushed his palm over the sweater.

"It's okay, Lane." She grasped his wrist and tugged so his hand rested on her stomach. Then she covered the back of his hand with her much smaller one.

Her stomach was harder than he'd imagined it would be. Not that she was *that* far along, but he'd just thought the bump would be softer. Losing himself in the moment, he started moving his hand so he could feel the place where his child was growing.

Evie leaned back and it seemed like the most natural thing in the world to shift so she could lean back against him. He reached his other hand to her stomach, so his arms were wrapped around her.

"Amazing," he whispered, resting his cheek against the top of her head.

"As soon as you can start feeling kicks from the outside, I'll let you know," she said in a soft voice.

He closed his eyes, breathing in the scent of her hair. With their hands cradling their growing baby, he could almost imagine that this moment was actually his life. That the dreams of a much younger him had actually come true instead of crumbling around him. He wanted to stay like this forever.

Then a phone vibrated and their bodies were pressed so close together, Lane couldn't tell if it was his phone in his front pocket or her phone in her back pocket. He dropped his hand to his side as Evie stepped forward, already missing the warmth of her body and the curve of her belly under his palm.

"They're probably wondering where I am." She pulled out her phone and smiled at the screen. "Mallory wants to know if I'm wandering around the orchard, hopelessly lost."

"Tell her you keep turning left at the tree with the red apples."

Evie laughed as she typed. "I'm telling her I'm almost there, and that you're with me so they don't need to worry."

"They might worry *more*, knowing we're out here together."

After tucking her phone back in her pocket, Evie started walking. "I don't know. Your mom was very quick to jump to my defense when my family didn't want me to walk. And based on the fact you had to have arrived not long after we did, she'd already called you and she knew you'd be here."

"You don't think my mom was *trying* to throw

us together, do you?" That didn't make any sense to him. Not once during any of Evie's trips back to Stonefield over the years had his mom hinted that he should go out with Evie again. She may have forgiven Evie for leaving her son, but she certainly hadn't forgotten it.

Of course Evie hadn't been carrying his child during any of those previous trips back to town.

"I doubt it," she said, giving him a sheepish grin. "She's not exactly my biggest fan. It was just really weird. But it doesn't matter. We're just two friends walking through an apple orchard together, right?"

Just two friends. He smiled, hoping it didn't look as forced as it felt, because that's what they'd been working toward. "Right. Just two friends wandering through the apple trees."

Gwen's advice had worked. They'd relaxed and stopped trying to force enjoying each other's company and now there they were, doing just that. That had been the goal—be friends so they could peacefully co-parent their child.

Yet somehow, right now, it just didn't feel like enough.

Chapter Nine

Mrs. Welch has asked us to thank the wonderful community of Stonefield for their generosity and to let you all know that she appreciates the "bushels and bushels" of apples she's found on her porch. They cheered her immensely and she'll spend as much time in the kitchen as her cast allows to make sure none of them go to waste.

—Stonefield Gazette *Facebook Page*

By Tuesday, Evie was practically itching to see Lane again. Even after they'd caught up with the family, the warmth between them had lingered, and they'd had a wonderful day together. Yesterday, she hadn't seen him at all, though. After he and Case were done with their jobs for the day, she knew Lane had been in the brewing cellar with Irish. She'd seen his truck. But she hadn't seen *him*, and they hadn't had a meeting last night because her mom had a headache and there was nothing particularly urgent on the agenda.

Today, she was alone in the house. Irish was in the brewing cellar and the boys were at school. Her mom and Mallory were at the thrift store, and Gwen was deep in writing and hadn't crossed the street to visit since they went apple picking. Evie was celebrating the solitude with a little housework, but at least she was doing the housework with her favorite playlist blasting from the Bluetooth speaker she was moving from room to room.

The music paused when her phone chimed, and she pulled it out of her back pocket to find a text from Molly, which she'd sent to the group chat that included Gwen and Mallory.

Lane went to library and checked out every book about childbirth and parenting they had.

Evie groaned, not wanting to think about how Molly had gotten that information. She didn't think people had really noticed the baby bump yet, thanks to it being autumn wardrobe season, but they would certainly notice Lane Thompson going into full fatherhood prepper mode.

A text came through from Gwen. Oh no. The last time I looked at that section (for book research, I promise!) they still had an ancient parenting book that said the safest way for a baby to ride in a car was in a basket on the floor behind the driver's seat.

Then Mallory chimed in. The library committee's been after Mrs. Denning to weed the collection for ages. Maybe when she retires in the spring, the new librarian will do it.

I'm pretty sure Lane knows car seats exist now, Evie typed.

Then came a question from Mallory that made Evie suck in a breath because it hadn't even crossed her mind.

Is Lane going to birthing classes with you?

Rather than give in to the urge to throw her phone across her room, Evie dropped it in her lap and pressed her hands to her cheeks. Having a baby was so complicated. Being in Stonefield and seeing Lane practically every day was so complicated.

Being in Stonefield and having a baby *with* Lane while seeing him practically every day? She wasn't even sure there was a word that encompassed how complicated that situation was. And that was before they shared that moment in the orchard.

I don't know who's going with me yet. It was the truth, since she hadn't even thought about it yet.

And she certainly hadn't asked anybody. I'm getting in the shower now. Bye.

She wasn't getting in the shower, but she didn't feel like having a lengthy conversation about her nonexistent birthing plan right now—especially a lengthy conversation that had to be typed into her phone. Laundry was next on her list, and it couldn't be put off. She couldn't comfortably wear over half of her wardrobe now, so she had to do laundry more often than she'd like.

She'd just set the basket on the floor in front of the washing machine when her phone chimed again and she groaned. Hopefully they weren't going to continue the conversation while she pretended to take a shower, leaving her who knew how many messages to catch up on later. But when she looked at the notification to see who'd missed the point of her shower lie, it wasn't from the group chat. The text message was from Lane, and Molly and her sisters weren't the only ones thinking about the baby today.

I have a book that says you're past the time when they can tell if the baby's a boy or a girl. Do you know? You'd tell me if you know, right?

She leaned against the washing machine, smiling at her phone as she typed in a response. Oh, did I forget to tell you I'm carrying triplets?

The three dots that indicated he was typing appeared, and then disappeared. Appeared. Disappeared. Evie managed to get her clothes and the detergent into the washer and started the wash cycle before her phone finally chimed with a response.

Great news! I can't wait to tell everybody we're having three babies! I'm going to call my mom right now.

Her eyes narrowed as she considered whether he might be serious. She didn't think so. Lane wasn't the sort to use exclamation marks in his text messages, so he'd probably used them deliberately because he was toying with her. But if she was wrong, everybody in her family was going to think she was having triplets by the time the washer hit the spin cycle.

He'd do it, too.

Don't you dare.

This time the three dots were replaced almost immediately by a new message. Do you know?

No. They asked me when I had my ultrasound, but I said I didn't want to know. Would you want to know?

I wish you'd asked me to go with you.

She wished it, too, but it was too late to change it. I'm sorry. We weren't really speaking at the time, and Mallory went with me. I didn't know they were going to do an ultrasound or I would have told you, but they wanted to confirm my due date. But you're invited to every future appointment. I'll text Laura when I make them.

Thank you. I'd like that.

We can probably still find out if you want to know.

The dots came and went several times before a response came through. What are you doing right now?

I just put in a load of wash.

I'm in the taproom, doing some cleaning. If you come over, we can talk about it without all the typing.

She shouldn't. Considering she'd spent the last two days obsessed with how good it had felt to have his arms wrapped around her again, she wasn't sure she should be alone with him.

On the other hand, there were conversations they needed to have that she'd rather not have her family involved in, and it wasn't easy to find the time or space to *be* alone around here. Successful co-parenting was not going to involve them getting along, but she was going to have to learn how to be around him without wishing things could be something they weren't.

I'll be right over.

After setting an alarm on her phone so she wouldn't forget she had clothes in the washing machine and have to wash them again by the time she finally realized it, she crossed the yard to the taproom and let herself in.

He was polishing one of the taps, and he was alone. "Is Irish downstairs?"

"Yeah, he'll be busy for a while yet, though, so we can talk."

"How come you're not at work?" she asked, sitting on one of the barstools. "I didn't hear your truck pull in."

"I'm not surprised you didn't hear the truck, since I could hear your music from outside. And today's job went faster than we thought it would, but we didn't have enough of the day left to do any of the others on the list, so we quit early."

"Ah." She smiled when he poured her an ice water and set it on a coaster in front of her. "Thanks. So, do you want to know if the baby's a boy or a girl?"

"I'm not sure," he said. "But the decision's kind of up to you by default."

"There are ways that you can be informed without me having to find out, you know."

He laughed, the rich sound echoing around the empty taproom. "You really think my mom, Ellen and your sisters would give me a second's peace if I knew the baby's gender?"

She shrugged. "So we don't tell them that you found out."

He considered that for a moment, his brow furrowing. "I don't want to be the only person who knows. I don't think it would be fun at all."

"Okay, so we either find out together or we wait."

"Are you leaning one way or the other?" he asked. "You already had an opportunity to find out and passed, so it seems like you don't want to know."

"I wasn't sure, in that moment. I wasn't expecting the ultrasound yet, so I hadn't thought about it and once you know, you can't un-know it."

"I feel like Mom and Ellen would want to know. They can get a head start on their knitting and all that."

"But what if they're wrong? Sometimes they are. They can still start knitting, just with more neutral colors."

He covered her hand with his, tipping his head so he could see her eyes. "My gut says you don't actually want to know. And I promise I'm okay, either way. I just wanted to know if you'd found out and hadn't told me."

"I wouldn't do that." She took a deep breath,

thought for a second and then exhaled slowly. "I think I want to wait."

He smiled. "Then we'll wait."

"A question that's going to come up—because I was already asked about it this morning—that you should think about is whether you're going to birthing classes with me." She sighed, hating how awkward it felt to talk to him about this. "Molly told us you'd gotten some books from the library, so it was an obvious question, I guess. You have plenty of time to think about it."

"I... I guess I hadn't really given it a lot of thought. Again, that's kind of your decision, since the person who's going to be in the room with you when you have the baby is the person who should go. There's your mom and your sisters to consider."

"You can be in the delivery room if you want to, Lane. No matter what, it's your baby and I'm okay with you being in there with me, so it's your decision. And you know my mom and my sisters will be in and out no matter who goes to the classes with me."

"If I miss it, I'll always regret it. I know I will."

"Then we'll do it together."

She realized his hand was not only still covering hers, but his fingers had slid between hers so they were *almost* holding hands.

When he looked down, she knew he was aware of it, too. For a long moment there was nothing but the fast beating of her heart and the sound of their breaths, and then he slowly pulled his hand away.

Friends, she reminded herself. More than anything, they needed to learn to be friends and she'd learned the hard way that giving in to heat still simmering between them didn't get them any closer to that goal.

Lane started talking about a winter ale he and Irish were planning, and Evie sighed because she recognized that he was trying to put some emotional distance between them. She cared passionately about the brewery as a family business, but she didn't really care about the making of the beer and he knew it. She let him ramble for a while, nodding and making the appropriate noises to show she was mostly paying attention, but eventually she got tired of sitting on the stool.

"I should get back to the house," she said when he finally ran out of things to say about the new ale. She slid off the barstool and grabbed her empty glass. "I've got a pretty epic to-do list today."

"I need to get downstairs and give Irish a hand. Just set the glass in there and I'll run it through later."

After setting the glass in an empty bus pan, Evie took a second to center herself. She was going to turn around and walk out, tossing a breezy goodbye in Lane's direction as she headed for the door. Then she was going to go in the house and not think about the weight of his hand covering hers or the way the lines of his face had softened as he looked at them.

But when she turned to leave, Lane was right there, setting his cleaning supplies down on the counter. His gaze dropped to the swell of her stomach and her resolve slipped when the corners of his mouth lifted slightly and his eyes warmed.

It had been hard enough to push her love for this man to the back of her mind over the years. This excited-to-be-a-dad version of him was making it impossible.

"If I'm going to birthing classes with you and I'm going to be in the delivery room, is it okay if I go to your checkup appointments with you, too?"

"As long as everything keeps going okay, there won't be many for a while, but of course you can go if you're free."

He smiled and her pulse quickened. "I'll be free."

She wasn't sure who moved first, but before she could even consider if it was a good idea or not—and it almost definitely wasn't—she was in his arms. Her hands pressed against his back, holding him to her as their lips met.

One of the few constants in her life was the incessant craving for Lane's kisses and his mouth on hers—demanding and hungry—filled some part of her that always felt empty. She relaxed against him as he cupped the back of her neck and the other hand slid up her side. Her nipples were taut, waiting for his touch.

Then an annoying dance tune startled them, and Lane broke off the kiss with a muttered curse.

"Does your phone have a Chaperone setting or what? First the apple orchard and now this?"

Trying to catch her breath, Evie pulled her phone from her back pocket and silenced it. "I set an alarm so I wouldn't forget to switch my laundry."

And it was probably a good thing she had because there were heavy footsteps crossing the taproom floor and she realized she hadn't heard Irish coming up the stairs or the beep when the electronic lock engaged behind him. Getting caught making out in the kitchen wasn't high on her list of fun things to do.

She moved away from Lane and, in doing so, ended up stepping out of the kitchen and into Irish's line of sight. He stopped walking and his gaze bounced between her and Lane, who'd followed her out.

"Hey, Evie." He tipped his hat. "I didn't realize you were here. I heard weird music for a second and thought Lane was playing with a radio."

"It was my alarm. We were just…talking about baby stuff, and I had a drink—water, obviously, because I can't have beer—and then I put my glass in the kitchen." She recognized that she was babbling and snapped her mouth shut.

"Okay," Irish said, nodding.

"I'm in the middle of doing laundry, so I should go."

And she did, practically fleeing the taproom. What had she done?

* * *

"You're whistling," Irish said. "That's new."

Lane hadn't even realized he was doing it while he restocked the coasters. "Guess I'm having a good day."

"Really?" Irish looked up from the bar he'd been polishing. The man took a great deal of pride in the gleaming surface. "That have anything to do with Evie?"

"What makes you think it has anything to do with her?"

"How about the fact I started to go upstairs, saw the two of you together and came back down here."

"Oh." Lane's face felt hot all of a sudden.

"Did you see…uh, what were we doing?"

Irish's eyebrow shot up. "You're kidding me. In the *taproom*?"

"Not *that*." Lane didn't necessarily want to kiss and tell, but he didn't want anybody thinking he was getting busy in their place of business, either. "There was a kiss. That's it."

Leaning against the wall, Irish pushed his hat back slightly—maybe so Lane could see the skepticism written all over his face—and crossed his arms. "I don't think there's any *that's it* when it comes to you and Evie."

"It was just a kiss." A kiss he'd felt to the very depths of his soul, but technically still just a kiss.

"Just a kiss that's got you whistling while you work."

Lane was saved from further conversation by Irish's phone chiming. He was starting to wonder how anybody got anything done with the phones interrupting all the time. Irish read a message and then Lane chuckled as he watched his friend scowling at the screen as he worked at typing in a response. He'd traded his old flip phone in for a smartphone shortly after marrying Mallory because so much of the communication about the brewery was done in an exhausting group text chain that probably needed its own server farm at this point. But he had big hands and text messages were still a chore for him.

As soon as he hit the Send button, though, the frown was gone and Irish grinned at him. "The store's slow, so my wife's coming home for…uh, a break. She needs me to help her with…something."

Lane laughed. "Gee, I wonder what that could be. Go. Help your wife with her something. I'm going to lock up and head home myself."

Hours later, when sleep evaded him because he couldn't stop replaying the kiss with Evie over and over in his mind, Lane got up and went downstairs to the kitchen. He wasn't into warm milk, but tossing and turning wasn't cutting it. He'd make a decaf for himself and maybe read a few pages of his book to distract his brain from thoughts of Evie, and then he'd try again.

He was halfway through the mug of decaf and hadn't even opened the book when his mom walked into the kitchen. She looked surprised to see him, since he didn't share her night owl tendencies. "What are you doing up?"

"I can't sleep."

On her way by, she ruffled his hair as though he was still a kid. "I told you not to read all those birthing books at once. You've got to space those out."

"It wasn't so much the reading as the looking at the pictures." When she laughed, he scrubbed his hands over his face. "Actually, it's not the books at all."

"Then what's keeping you awake?"

He shrugged one shoulder, not sure he wanted to talk about it. Plus, it was hard to put into words things he hadn't even been able to mentally sort through yet.

"Wild guess," his mom said as she pulled out a chair and sat across from him. "It's Evie keeping you from sleeping?"

"Kind of, but not Evie and me so much as Evie and the baby. I spend a lot of time trying to figure out where I'll fit in there and what my life's going to look like."

"What do you *want* it to look like?"

He frowned. "You could have eased into the hard questions, Ma."

"It's late. I don't have the time or the energy to dance around the real question."

The problem was that the answer to *that* question was impossible. He wanted his life to be full because his wife never divorced him and they were living happily-ever-after. He'd already lost that and he couldn't get it back.

"Okay," Laura said when he didn't answer. "Let's back it up. When you picture yourself with a baby, is Evie there, too?"

He was tempted to make a snarky remark about it being hard to have the baby without the mother, but he didn't because he knew what she really meant. When he pictured himself watching a football game with his baby sleeping on his chest, was Evie cuddled against his side?

"It's not a secret I've never gotten over Evie. But the fact we irritate each other is also not a secret."

"I told you years ago it would take time. Maybe it's time."

"You were talking about me getting over her."

"Maybe you just assumed I was." She smiled when he gave her a *really, Mom?* look. "Everybody in town is excited about the baby."

He sat up straighter in his chair. "What do you mean? How does everybody in town know?"

She laughed. "What a question. For one, the people in this town have eyes and can see that Evie's pregnant. The rest...well, it's Stonefield."

"Nobody's said anything to me."

"Of course not. That would be rude, since you haven't said anything publicly."

Lane rubbed the spot between his eyebrows with the side of his thumb. This town was really something else. "I should get some sleep. Case and I have that big job you scheduled that's going to take us a solid couple of days, and that's if we work late. If we didn't have Irish at the brewery now, I'd be screwed."

"If you didn't have Irish, I probably wouldn't have scheduled the job," she pointed out. "I don't want you up in the bucket, running chain saws with no sleep, so good night."

He kissed the top of her head as he passed by and went upstairs. He'd go to bed, but he wasn't so sure he'd be getting a good night's sleep. Not when his mind wanted to fill his head with images of what could have happened in the taproom kitchen if Evie's phone hadn't interrupted them.

Someday he was going to learn that he couldn't get within arm's reach of his ex-wife when they were alone or they'd end up touching that hot stove and burning themselves again because they never seemed to learn.

Today hadn't been that day.

Chapter Ten

If you have a craving for Mrs. Welch's blue-ribbon-winning apple butter, stop by Dearborn's Market for a jar today! Mrs. Welch canned up more than she has room to store, so all of the extras are available to buy at the market, with half the proceeds going toward her medical bills and half to the town's Helping Hands fund. You'll also find applesauce, apple tarts and apple muffins if you hurry!
—Stonefield Gazette *Facebook Page*

Evie found a parking space close to Sutton's Seconds but she didn't climb out of the Wrangler right away. She wasn't particularly excited about this shopping trip and she'd even tried to drag Gwen away from her keyboard. It hadn't worked.

She needed maternity clothes. Mallory had been dropping hints for days, trying to tempt her with the promise of at least a few cute tops, but Evie had been in denial. She didn't want to spend money on clothes she would only wear for a few months. She did, however, like being able to move and breathe, and she didn't want to smoosh the baby.

After browsing a few online stores to scope out the latest in pregnancy fashion, she was left with two choices—rob a bank or hit up her mom's shop. She knew both bank tellers and she was pretty sure they'd turn her in, so secondhand it was.

Walking through the shop's door felt like home almost as much as walking through the front door of the actual house did. She hadn't liked working in the store as a teen, but she was pretty sure she'd taken her first steps here.

The shelves and racks were always full. The stock was a mix of donations, things Ellen and Laura found to buy and resell and items being sold on consignment, and so varied that no matter what a resident of Stonefield was looking for, Sutton's Seconds was their first stop. And Ellen had pretty high standards, so hopefully she'd find the cute maternity clothes she'd been promised.

"Evie!" Her mom's face lit up when she saw her walk in, and it brightened Evie's mood considerably. "You finally came."

"Unless togas are forecasted to be the next hot fashion trend in Stonefield and there are extra bedsheets on hand, I didn't really have a choice. And I guess I should start thinking about what I'll need to buy before the baby's born."

"You need to make a list of what you'd like to have new and what can be secondhand."

Evie laughed. "You've owned this thrift store our entire lives, Mom. I'm good with secondhand."

"I know you are, honey. But this is your first baby and that's special. Plus, we'll need that list for your baby shower anyway."

"Oh good, you're here." Mallory joined them by the counter, and she looked excited to help her sister shop. "We've got a lot of maternity and baby things in right now, and I saved a few things out back, too. It's too bad you're having a January baby because we have the cutest maternity sundresses."

"Maternity sundresses sound comfortable." Evie sighed. "Do you have maternity cardigans, because I could make a layered look work."

"And maternity tights?" Mallory snorted. "I think you'd be better off buying winter clothes for winter."

"Fine. Lead the way."

Evie was surprised to find enough things she liked in her size so that, other than underwear and a few sweaters and some warm loungewear, she wouldn't have to order many things new. And enough customers went in and out so Evie got to spend a little one-on-one time with Mallory. Even though they lived in the same house, they were seldom alone.

"How's married life?" she asked while they were perusing the baby furniture aisle, and she was pleased to see Mallory's cheeks flush. That was a very good sign, as far as she was concerned.

"It's good. We're, uh…" She paused and looked around to see if anybody—probably their mother, in particular—was within earshot. "We're trying to get pregnant."

Evie had to slap her hand over her mouth to stifle the squeal of excitement. "That's so exciting, Mal. I didn't know you were going to try."

She shrugged. "I mean, it's okay if we don't. Irish loves those boys like they're his own and we'll be a very happy family, just the four of us. And I shouldn't say we're *trying*, I guess. We're just not trying *not* to, if you know what I mean."

"I thought maybe you wouldn't want to start over now that the boys can get their own cereal in the morning."

"I never thought I'd want another baby, but I really do."

Evie ran her hand over her stomach. "It would be so amazing if you got pregnant. And Gwen, too. Then this kid would have cousins to play with. I mean, I love Jack and Eli, but if I tell them to play with their cousin, they'll probably stick the baby in a backpack and go ride their bikes. And I don't mean a real baby carrier type of backpack."

Mallory laughed. "I'd like to say you're wrong, but…yeah. It would be pretty cool, so fingers crossed."

"What are you girls laughing about back here?"

That was all the warning they got before Ellen turned the corner, and Evie gave her an innocent look. "Nothing much. We were imagining Jack and Eli as babysitters."

"Oh…no. I think I'll handle that for a while." She sank into the glider rocker they'd stuck at the end of the aisle, and which Evie had her eye on. "It's been busy today."

"Customers are a good thing," Mallory pointed out.

Evie silently agreed. Even though the brewery and taproom were doing really well, the thrift shop and the rent from the apartment above it were not only her mom's primary income, but had provided for Mallory and the boys, as well. Now that Irish had bought into Sutton's Place, things were definitely easier, but Ellen had inherited the business from her parents and despite having changed its name a long time ago, it was personal for her.

Ellen nodded, but she looked thoughtful. "Laura asked me to go away with her next weekend, but I don't know if I should."

"Where does she want to go?" Mallory asked before Evie could.

"North Conway. It seems like a waste of money to pay for a hotel room that's not even two hours from home, but the fall foliage will be gorgeous."

"You'll never get a hotel room at this time of year, though," Evie said. "In North Conway during peak leaf-peeping season? Not a chance."

"Laura said she reserved a room months ago, but she didn't want to give me enough advance notice to overthink my way out of going."

Her mom's best friend definitely knew her well, Evie thought. "You should totally go. You haven't gone away anywhere in forever, and you and Laura would have such a good time."

"I don't know," Ellen said, scowling at her tea-cup. "Who would take care of the boys?"

Mallory raised her hand. "That would be me, since I'm their mother and all."

Ellen chuckled. "Sorry, honey. I didn't mean that the way it came out. I just meant that if you're with Jack and Eli, who's going to run the kitchen?"

Evie raised her hand for a few seconds. "Mom, we have more than enough people to make the tap-room run, even if Mal takes the weekend off to be with the boys."

"I just hate the idea of everybody having to work harder so I can look at the foliage. It's not like the leaves don't change color here in Stonefield."

"This is why Laura didn't give you months to talk yourself out of going," Evie teased. "Go. Have fun."

When her mother's eyes welled up with tears, Evie grimaced and looked at Mallory. When her sister sighed and gave her a sad smile, she knew they were on the same page. Ellen's reluctance to go away probably had very little to do with who was going to make the nachos and wash the glasses.

"It's time, Mom," Mallory said softly. "You told me that you and your grief therapist have talked about it being time for you to discover who you are without Dad—that you filled space he left in your life with the brewery that meant so much to him, and with having Gwen and Evie home. But you need to live *your* life, Mom. Dad would want you to go leaf-peeping with Laura and you know it."

Ellen smiled and swiped at the tears on her cheeks. "If he was still here, he'd want me to go off with Laura so he wouldn't feel guilty about locking himself in the brewing cellar and ignoring me."

They all laughed because it was true, and Evie was relieved to see some of the emotional strain ease from her mother's face. Then the bell over the door rang and she pushed herself out of the rocker.

"If you see something you want that won't fit in your Jeep, we'll put it out back for now."

"I really like that rocker. I get a family discount right?" She gave her mom her most angelic smile.

Her mom snorted. "Twenty percent off. You know that."

Evie sighed as her mom walked away, and then she looked at the price tag and winced. She already had a chair in her room, even though it didn't rock, and the newborn-preparedness shopping list was already going to have her looking for change in the couch cushions, so 20 percent off wasn't going to be enough.

"I'll put it out back," Mallory told her. "We'll have an unofficial registry list here at the shop for your shower."

"That's a pretty big gift, Mal."

"Maybe it'll be a joint gift." She nudged Evie with her elbow. "Or maybe Lane will buy it for you."

"Lane's not going to be at my baby shower."

Mallory shrugged. "He might. That's a thing now, you know. Guys go to baby showers. And even if he doesn't, he'd buy it for you. I think he'd buy you anything you want."

"He's going to help pay for stuff for the baby, but he's not responsible for me."

"I'm not saying he *has* to. I think he'll *want* to."

Evie caught her meaning and wanted to drive home and march down to the cellar so she could kick her brother-in-law in the shin. "What has Lane told Irish that makes you think that?"

"Dammit." Mallory looked guilty. "Nothing. I was just… I mean, anybody can see the way you two look at each other."

"So Lane didn't tell Irish who then told you that he and I kissed in the taproom's kitchen?"

Her sister's eyes widened. "You kissed him?"

"Shh! I really don't want Mom in on this conversation. And you didn't know that?"

"No, I didn't know. Irish and I talk sometimes

about how you two are obviously still hot for each other, but if Lane told Irish about the kissing, he didn't tell me."

"Great. I confessed for no reason." It was a bit of a relief, though. It wasn't as if everybody couldn't tell they still had chemistry since she was waddling around with the results on display for everyone to see, and now she could talk to her sister about it, at least.

"I think it's wonderful," Mallory said, her face softening. "Imagine if we not only had babies around the same age, but we were married to three guys who are really good friends. It would be perfect."

Right. *That* was the reason she hadn't intended to kiss and tell—because then the people around them would have expectations, especially with a baby on the way. "We did the married thing once already, remember? It didn't work out."

Mallory waved her hand. "That was then. You've both grown and changed so much."

"We do manage to be in the same room together for more than five minutes without arguing now," Evie admitted. "Sometimes."

"See? It's like you're meant to be together."

They made it four days, Lane thought as he refused to yield in what felt very much like a staring contest with Evie. Four days from kissing in the taproom kitchen to her looking as if she wanted to set him on fire with her eyeballs.

And all he'd done was tell her one of their regular customers was selling a late-model crossover that would be safe, good in the snow and still sporty looking, and he was letting it go for a very reasonable price.

She definitely wasn't taking it well.

"I'm not selling my Wrangler," she said in a voice that let him know in no uncertain terms this conversation was over.

But it wasn't over. He couldn't let it go. "I know you love it, but it's not very practical when it comes to an infant."

"Maybe you two want to take a break right now," Irish said, leaning past Lane to reach the tap. "I've got the bar and Mal can cover the tables for a few minutes."

Lane could see that Evie wanted to argue, but Irish hadn't phrased it as a question. After blowing out an exasperated breath, she spun on her heel and walked toward the door. Arguing with Evie in the yard hadn't been on the list of things Lane wanted to do anytime soon, but when he glanced at Irish to say he didn't need a break, the cowboy gave him a stern look and tipped his head toward the door.

Of course Evie was leaned against the Wrangler when he got outside. She had her legs crossed at the ankles and her arms folded above the baby bump. Everything about her body language said she had zero interest in hearing what he had to say.

"What are you doing, Lane?" she demanded as

soon as he reached her. "We were in a good place. We were almost even friends again, and now you have to do this?"

"By *this*, you mean worrying about the safety of my child? Because that's a thing I'm always going to do, whether you and I are friends or not."

"And you think I'm not?"

"I don't know what you're thinking because you refuse to have a conversation about it."

"You telling me what I can and can't do is not a conversation."

"That's not what I'm doing."

"I have a mother and two older sisters. I know when I'm being bossed around." She rolled her eyes. "And you need to make up your mind because right now you're talking about safety, but a few minutes ago it was about bring practical."

"It's a soft top," he said, waving a hand at the vehicle behind her. "And look, I know it's safe enough. And if you want to try to climb in and out of the backseat with a baby carrier, that's on you. I can't make you do a damn thing, *obviously*, but that's not going to stop me from trying to make things easier for you."

"I can't buy a car right now, Lane," she said, and he could see how much she hated making that admission to him. "And, *no*—"

He froze with his hand in the air and his mouth open to speak.

"Don't you dare tell me you can help me buy a

car," she finished. He snapped his mouth shut. "I will never sell that Jeep. I love that thing with my whole heart. But since you won't leave it alone, the car seat is being installed in my mom's car for a while, not that it's any of your business."

"And Ellen's going to be able to climb in and out of that Jeep?"

She arched an eyebrow at him. "I dare you to go in that house right now and tell her you don't think she's capable of doing that."

"Nope." He was no fool. "But why didn't you just tell me that you already had a plan?"

"Because, *again*, it's not your business what I drive as long as the car seat is secure and the vehicle is safe."

She had a point. "But if you'd told me, despite it not being my business, we wouldn't be standing outside the bar having an argument right now."

As he watched, some of the stiffness went out of her spine, until she was more slumped against the Jeep than leaned against it. And there was a defeat in her expression he didn't like at all. "If it wasn't my Jeep, it would be something else. It's what we do, Lane."

"No." He wasn't going to give up on the good thing they'd been building. "That's what we *did*. We're doing better. You said yourself we're almost friends again. Almost friends who kissed just a few days ago, I might add."

"And yet look where we are now."

"Look, I'm sorry I told you about the car for sale and pushed back against your Wrangler. I shouldn't have tried to interfere with you like that." He was going to have to give up on the assertions he had the right to an opinion about the vehicles his child rode in if they were going to have peace. "But a little argument doesn't mean we're failing at being friends, Evie. We're going to disagree a lot in the coming years, I'm sure, but we're getting better at disagreeing."

She didn't look convinced. "How do you figure that?"

"Well, you haven't left town yet," he pointed out, and they both laughed.

But it didn't last long, because she slid a hand over her stomach. "I can't really leave now, can I?"

The question hit Lane like a glass of ice water tossed in his face, reminding him that no matter how well they got along, Evie didn't want to be here. She'd come back to Stonefield because she didn't want to have a baby without the love and support of her family.

He wasn't a part of that—if he'd factored into her decision at all, he'd probably been in the cons column—and it sounded to him like she was doing her best to keep it that way. Sure, she might say all the right things about being friends and co-parenting, but when it really came down to it, she'd get prickly and put that distance between them again.

"So we're good?" she asked, pushing herself away from the Jeep.

"Yeah." She was right—this was just the way it was between them. "We're good."

Maybe this was as good as it could be, and he was going to have to learn to live with that.

Chapter Eleven

Stonefield PD fielded multiple reports last night about screaming shortly after midnight, which many of you have been talking about in our comments. After a brief investigation, the officer on duty determined the screaming sound was made by a saw cutting the High Street sign post off at the ground. We asked Chief Bordeaux for an official statement and we offer his comment in its entirety:

"Now they stole the whole damn sign? I quit."

Don't worry, Stonefield. The Board of Selectmen's secretary assures us our chief of police has not submitted a letter of resignation.

—Stonefield Gazette *Facebook Page*

Ellen and Laura hadn't even been gone two hours when Evie got a phone call from her mom. "Can you do us a huge favor?"

"If you're going to tell me you're afraid you left the oven on, I'm going to laugh at you."

"Laura left the hotel information on a sticky note in her office and she can't find the confirmation email on her phone, so she might have deleted it. Can you go over to the house and get it for us?"

"The hotel will have you in the computer, you know."

"There are a *lot* of hotels in North Conway."

Evie sighed and rested her forehead against her hand. "You don't remember which hotel?"

"She made the reservation months ago, and she thought she knew, but they all have very similar names."

"Okay. Did she call Lane, since he actually lives in the same house as the note?"

"Of course she did, but he's not answering."

"Fine. I'll go now and call you once I'm in the office."

When she got to the Thompson house, she didn't see Lane's truck and the front door was locked. After grabbing the not-so-hidden spare key, she let herself in and made her way to Laura's office, trying not to think about the fact that the last time she'd been in this house, she'd ended up in Lane's bed. Smiling as she ran her hand over her swollen stomach, she told herself Lane not being around was for the best.

The sticky note with the information about the hotel was right in the center of Laura's desk—probably so she wouldn't forget to take it—and Evie called her mom to give her the information. She also snapped a picture of the note and sent it to her, just in case. She was about to leave when a framed photo on the end of the desk caught her attention and she froze.

They'd cropped her out.

She picked up the frame and looked at what had probably been the last family photo taken before Lane's dad died. Lane and his parents were laughing at the camera and it was one of the happiest pictures she'd ever seen. But she knew why Lane's right arm went out of the frame.

That's where Evie had been. They'd been holding hands, only a month or so after their wedding, and the four of them had gone to the Old Home Day celebration together. Her father had taken the picture after cracking some ridiculous dad joke that made them all laugh.

And they'd deliberately cut her out of it. It shouldn't hurt as much as it did.

"What are you doing, Evie?"

The scream was out of her mouth before her brain could register that it was Lane's voice and she whirled to face him with the hand clutching the photo flying to her chest and the other sliding over her small baby bump. He looked and sounded angry, but she watched the slight softening in the lines of his face when his gaze tracked the movement.

"Lane!" Her heart was still hammering in her chest. "That wasn't nice."

He shrugged. "I don't really feel a need to be nice to people who break into my house."

She snorted. "It's not like I'm a burglar."

"Actually, you are." He gave a pointed glance to the picture frame in her hand.

Flustered, Evie put the photo back in its proper place and took one deep breath before turning to face him again. "I wasn't stealing it. I was just... looking at it."

Would he guess that she'd picked it up because she'd realized they'd cropped her out of the photo?

"Why are you wandering around our office?"

"Your mother forgot the sticky note she wrote the hotel information on, and thinks she probably deleted the confirmation email because she can't find it on her phone. She couldn't get hold of you, so they called and asked me to come over and get it."

"You could have knocked."

"I didn't see your truck and the door was locked, so I assumed you weren't home."

"My truck's in the garage because I was changing the oil and the door was locked to keep people from wandering around while I'm folding laundry with my earbuds in."

"I didn't actually *break* in, you know. The spare

key's been in the same place since we were kids, and Laura asked me to come in." She lifted her chin and started across the room. "And now I'm leaving."

He stuck out his arm to block her from leaving. "Should I frisk you before I let you leave?"

Evie assumed he was just being a smart-ass, until she glanced at his face to tell him to go to hell and saw the way he was looking at her. His gaze raked over her body and there was so much heat in that look, she was surprised it didn't singe her clothes right off her body.

"Don't look at me like that if you don't mean it," she warned. She didn't have the strength to resist him, so if they were going to avoid ending up in his bed again, it was on him.

"Oh, I mean it."

Evie put her hand on his chest, intending to exert just enough pressure to protect the space between them. As soon as her fingers splayed over the hard muscle, though, she remembered how much she loved touching his body. She put her other hand over his heart and then ran them outward, over his strong shoulders.

She didn't realize she'd failed at the distance-keeping and they were close enough to kiss until his mouth was on hers. The kiss was hard—almost punishing—and her fingertips bit into his upper arms as her knees went weak.

He broke off the kiss with a guttural growl. "Why can't I stop wanting you?"

Evie didn't want him to think about that right now. She wanted his mouth on hers again. She wanted his hands on her body, and she knew just how to distract him.

She scraped her nails up the back of his neck before burying her fingers in his hair and pulling his face to hers. She controlled the kiss this time, nipping at his bottom lip before sliding her tongue over his.

They were wearing too many clothes, thanks to the weather, but she didn't want to give him a chance to realize he was slowly backing her toward the desk. She indulged in a momentary fantasy of him sweeping the desk clean and taking her right there. But that was a lot of hard surface and edges for a pregnant woman, and Laura would straight-up murder them when she got home.

Lane broke off the kiss, running his thumb over her bottom lip. "I want you, Evie."

"I'm too pregnant to have sex on a hardwood floor," she told him, and was rewarded with a crooked grin.

"Want to go upstairs and fool around?"

The question—the same question he'd asked her back in high school whenever they managed to hang out without his parents around, with that same cooked grin—caused a nostalgic pang that almost killed the mood, but then his hand cupped the back of her neck and he kissed her. It was slow and a little sweet, and she absolutely wanted to go upstairs and fool around.

"Lead the way," she whispered.

He threaded his fingers through hers, holding her hand with a grip that made her wonder if he was afraid she'd change her mind and bolt for the door. They went up the stairs and she shivered as she crossed the threshold into his room.

Finally, she thought when he turned and hauled her into his arms. Evie lost herself in his kiss, and she stretched her arms around his neck to hold him close. His hands ran down her back and over the curve of her ass as his mouth left hers and made a hot trail over her jaw and down her neck.

He didn't seem to be in a hurry to get to the bed, but instead took his time kissing her as they slowly lost layers of clothing. As the peeling away revealed skin, she ran her hands over him, reveling in the familiar feel of his body. The taut muscles. Rough hands. Old scars. He'd worked hard his entire life and his body showed it.

"I've been thinking about this," he murmured against the skin revealed when he slid her bra strap down. "It's really *all* I think about."

"I'm so glad I decided to burgle your house tonight."

Chuckling, he swept her into his arms and carried her to the bed. As he lowered her, she reached out and grabbed the covers to yank them back. His mouth claimed hers as her back hit the mattress, but as soon as she was settled, he peeled off her leggings and underwear. He even managed to get her socks off in that one pull, which impressed her.

Even more impressive was the look she got at him when he stripped off his boxer briefs and tossed them aside. While he wasn't all hard rippled muscle because he liked food a lot and had a bit of a thing for desserts, working hard kept him in shape. He was a little broader now than he'd been ten years ago, and stronger, and she rolled onto her side so she could grab his arm and tug him down next to her.

He kissed her again, then he blazed a path down her neck with his tongue. She moaned when he lavished that same attention on her breasts, his tongue circling her sensitive nipples until she squirmed. Then he ran his hand over the curve of her stomach and stilled.

He looked down at her body, and smiled. "The last time you were in this bed, I didn't think it was possible for you to be any sexier. I was so wrong."

She raked her fingernails up his back, loving the way he shivered. "And you can't hurt the baby. Just so you know."

"What do you think I really wanted to know when I checked all those books out of the library?" he teased, and she laughed as he rolled her onto her back.

But when he pressed a kiss to her rounded stomach before his lips traveled lower, the laughter turned into a needy moan. When he pushed her knees apart and buried his mouth between her thighs, her back arched and her fingers tightened in his hair.

Evie lost herself in the sensation of his mouth and his fingers, and he didn't stop until the much-needed orgasm washed over her. She said his name as her fingers fisted in the sheets, and when the waves had passed and she was trying to catch her breath, he nipped at her thigh before kissing his way back up her body.

"I can't wait anymore, Evie. You're so… I can't."

"I don't want you to."

He sank into her, filling her completely, and she moaned as he moved—slowly and almost gently at first—but she knew he was on the edge. She slid her hands over his hips, urging him on as he thrust faster and deeper. The friction was delicious and she closed her eyes.

"Evie," he said in a voice that was little more than a groan.

He was close, and she reached down to stroke her clit because she was, too. His muscles trembled under her other hand, and she knew he was trying to hold it back. Then he fisted his hand in her hair and the orgasm crashed into her, stealing her breath, and he let himself go. With a ragged moan, he thrust hard enough to make her gasp and then collapsed, sliding a little to the side so his weight wasn't on her belly.

He kissed her jaw and her temple, then her shoulder, before dropping his head to the pillow. His breath came in hot gusts against her cheek and she turned her head to kiss his forehead.

They stayed like that until Lane's body relaxed to the point she was afraid he was going to fall asleep and if that happened, she was going to lose all circulation in her arm. It was trapped under his body and she wasn't sure had the leverage to pull it free.

"I'm going to go get a drink," she whispered, and that wasn't just an excuse. She was parched.

"I'll go grab you some water. Stay here." Lane was up and pulling on his boxer briefs before she could tell him she was fine, and she smiled as he hustled out the door. It was sweet, the way he was so determined to take care of her.

After a long stretch, complete with a sigh of contentment, Evie sat up with the sheet pulled over her breasts and looked around.

This hadn't been their room when they lived together in this house. It had still been his parents' room and they'd shared his childhood bedroom down the hall. Sometime over the last ten years, they'd converted the extra family room downstairs into a bedroom and bathroom for his mom, and the formal dining room into an office, and Lane had moved into this room.

They'd conceived their child in this room, she thought with a smile.

She noticed a photo frame facedown on his nightstand and nosiness got the better of her. She crawled to his side of the bed and lifted it, tilting it so she could see the picture in the light coming through the window. Then she pressed a hand to her mouth, stifling the sob that wanted to break free.

It was the same photo that was framed on his mother's desk. Except in this one, his parents were the ones cropped out and it was a close-up of Evie and Lane, their hands joined as they laughed at the camera. The memory of that day—the joy and love and absolute perfection of her life—was so strong she could barely breathe.

And he kept this next to his bed.

Facedown, she thought. She didn't remember him reaching for his nightstand at all, which meant it had been like this when they walked in. Did he look at it sometimes? Or did it just sit there, their faces hidden from his view?

Why not put it in a drawer? Or throw it away? Why keep this photo next to his bed in such a way he couldn't actually see it?

The idea he was torturing himself somehow with the memory of that day made her heart ache in her chest. After carefully putting the frame back the way she'd found it, she slid off the bed and gathered her clothes. The contentment that had made her muscles languid was gone, replaced by the familiar guilt and shame, and her movements were jerky as she pulled her bra and panties on.

She was yanking her sweater over her head when

Lane walked into the bedroom, carrying two bottles of water. "What are you doing?"

"I'm getting dressed so I can go home." She yanked the sweater down and grabbed her leggings. Putting them on standing up was out of the question, so she took them to the chair and sat. "This was a mistake, Lane, and we both know it."

When she'd pushed her feet through the leggings and stood to yank them over her butt, she realized he hadn't responded and looked up.

He'd definitely heard her. His jaw was clenched and the look in his eyes shook her to her core because she'd expected to him to be mad and make some cutting comment about her running away. But he looked confused and hurt, and the guilt she'd been carrying for ten years swelled to a whole new level.

She looked around for her phone—an excuse to look anywhere but back at him—before remembering it was downstairs in her coat pocket. He still hadn't said anything, and she didn't think there really was anything they *could* say, so she forced herself to walk out of his room. She made it down the stairs before the tears started, but her vision was blurring as she pulled on her coat and shoved her feet into her boots.

Stepping out into the cold air so soon after being in his warm bed made her suck in a breath, and she swiped at her eyes. She needed to get herself together if she was going to be able to see to drive home, or she was going to end up sitting in her Jeep in Lane's driveway while she cried herself out.

They were so perfect together, but obviously only in the bedroom, and she'd messed everything up. Again. Her need for him had made her forget that she was no good for him and that this was where they always ended up.

With Evie hurting him. Over and over again.

He was never going to learn.

Lane was so still, he felt the vibration of the front door of the old house closing. She was gone. Once again, he'd let Evie get close and—once again—she was taking off. And he'd never really understood her reasons, but this time it made no sense at all.

Something had happened while he was in the bathroom and he needed to know what. And this time, he wasn't going to get let her go without talking about it. He was tired of feeling helpless and resentful as she walked out the door, and if things were really going to change between them, it had to start now.

He dropped the water bottles and sprinted through the house and out the front door, desperate to catch her before she got in her Jeep. The cold made him very aware he was wearing nothing but boxer briefs, but if he'd taken the time to throw on sweats, she would have been gone. Instead, she was fishing her keys out of her coat pocket.

"Evie," he called, and when she turned to face

him, he could see the tears on her cheeks. Why was she crying when she was the one who'd left? "Come back inside."

"I'm going home, Lane."

"Talk to me first. Talk to me for a few minutes and then you can go."

"What is the point? You know—"

"Yes, I know. We're no good for each other. So you've said. Give me five minutes."

Evie shook her head, but he could see that she was wavering. "It's too cold for you to be out here in your underwear."

"Then come back inside."

"That's probably not a great idea."

He folded his arms across his chest. "Then we'll talk here."

She blew out an exasperated breath. "Fine. Talk."

"What happened in the two minutes I was gone? You were fine and then you weren't."

"You know we're not good for each other."

"We have a complicated history, sure, but I don't think that's what's going on here." He sighed. "Look, I came out here because in the past I've let you leave and just been angry about it and I don't want to do that anymore. I came after you, so now it's your turn to try something different and actually talk to me instead of just telling me we're no good for each other and walking away."

She looked like she was going to refuse and walk away, but after biting her bottom lip for a few seconds, she surrendered. "Why do you keep a picture of us facedown on your nightstand?"

He stilled, losing himself in her blue eyes as he absorbed the impact of the question.

He didn't want to talk about that. It would be easier to go back in the house and slam the door, letting her be mad at him forever, than to try to explain the photo.

But if he truly wanted to change the dynamic between them, then they needed to talk through some things. That's why he'd run outside in his underwear, after all. He'd thought they were going to talk about *her* issues, though. Not his.

"I keep it facedown on my nightstand because it hurts to look at it, but I can't bring myself to get rid of it or even shove it in a drawer because that also hurts. I can't look at how happy we were, but I can't let go of it, so it just sits there like that."

She didn't say anything. She just looked up at him with tears shimmering in her eyes, and he wondered if he'd done the right thing in coming after her. Maybe letting her go reopened old wounds each time it happened, but opening himself up emotionally this way and waiting to see how she would react was a fresh, much sharper pain.

"I always hurt you, Lane," she finally said in such a low voice he had to lean in to hear her. "Hurting you hurts *me*, and I can't keep doing it."

"We're not going to keep doing it. I didn't let you go and you talked to me instead of leaving, and now we're going to go back inside and celebrate this turning point in our relationship. Preferably by drinking something warm because I lost feeling in my extremities about thirty seconds after I walked out the door."

Her laughter was a balm to his ragged emotions, and she took the hand he held out. "I can't believe you're out here in boxer briefs for anybody to see."

Getting in the house and closing the door behind them was a blessed relief—not only because he'd only been slightly exaggerating about his frozen status, but because Evie had come back inside with him.

He cheated and microwaved water for hot cocoa because the chill had settled in, and curling up on the couch with Evie, a hot drink and a fleece throw was the only way he was going to warm up. Once they were settled in the living room and he'd had a few sips, he stopped shivering, at least.

She pulled out her phone and, after a few taps on the screen, she held it out to him. "This one is mine. The photo that hurts to look at, but that I can't delete."

He recognized the moment immediately. He'd just made the trip home from Montana for the last time, and Evie had run out of the house to greet him. He'd lifted her off her feet and his mom had snapped the picture at that moment. Evie had her hands braced on his shoulders and her hair was flying as he swung her up. The unmistakable love and joy on their faces hit him like a fist to the chest.

His mom had taken the photo with her camera and the original had been a print she'd picked up at the drug store. That meant somewhere along the line, Evie had either digitized her copy or had taken a photo of the picture so she could carry it with her on her phone.

"So you get it," he said quietly, referring to the photo of them on his nightstand.

"I get it." Then she twitched and her mouth curved into a smile. "This baby either really loves or really hates hot cocoa."

"What do you mean? Is it heartburn? We probably have something in the medicine cabinet." He set his mug down and started to get up, but she grabbed his wrist and tugged him closer to her.

"Here, you might finally be able to feel it." She pressed his hand over the side of her stomach. "Just wait."

A few seconds later, he felt the kick against his palm and sucked in a breath. "Evie."

"Isn't it amazing? I've been waiting for the kicks to be strong enough for you to feel."

He looked up at her, confused for a second when she was blurry, but then he realized there was a sheen of tears in his eyes and blinked them away. "That's our baby."

"Yes, it is. And feeling feisty, I might add."

The baby kicked his palm two more times before settling down, and Lane reluctantly pulled his hand away. "Does that happen a lot?"

"Sometimes. At first it was fluttering, but they've been getting stronger. Mallory assures me it won't be long before the baby's trying to rearrange my organs and kicking off anything I set on my stomach."

He chuckled, taking a sip of his hot cocoa as he rearranged the blanket around his legs. "I have vague memories of Mallory pleading with Eli to stop kicking her bladder."

Evie rolled her eyes, but she was smiling. "I can't wait."

He was quiet for a moment, and then he drew in a deep breath. Maybe it was the pictures and the breakthrough they'd had in communicating. Maybe it was the baby. And maybe it was sitting with her like this, cuddled in blankets and sipping hot cocoa.

Whatever it was, he knew he didn't want her to go. "Stay with me tonight, Evie."

Her gaze locked with his, and he could practically feel her blue eyes boring into his soul, as if trying to figure out what had triggered the invitation. He was about to reassure her it wasn't because they'd just bonded over the baby kicking. He *wanted* her.

But before he could come up with the right words, she sighed and gave him a small smile. "I'm going to have to text Mal and tell her I'm not coming home and where I am or she'll be worried. And then it's going to be a whole *thing* my family will want to stick their noses into."

He arched an eyebrow. "Did you tell her where you were going?"

"Yeah, but nobody thought you were home, remember?"

"I'm pretty sure she'll figure it out." He chuckled. "And if she doesn't, Irish will clue her in."

"Good point." She set her phone on the coffee table and then slid her hand under the blanket so it rested on his thigh. "You know, I bet I could warm you up faster than that hot cocoa can."

Lane set the mug next to her phone and grinned. "Challenge accepted."

Chapter Twelve

Mark your calendars, Stonefield! On October 28th, Sutton's Place Brewery & Tavern will be throwing a Halloween party! Wear a costume and you'll get half off from 7pm to closing. (As always, coffee and soda are free for designated drivers.) Dearborn's Market has donated three $25 gift cards to be awarded for Best Costume, Best Couple's Costume and Best Designated Driver Costume! While the party is for adults, they'll be giving out candy at the door to any kids who want to trick-or-treat early, so it'll be fun for everybody!

And don't forget to stop by tonight for Comedy Night! It's an open mic, so polish

up your best jokes and get ready to tickle
some funny bones!
　　　　—Stonefield Gazette *Facebook Page*

"So there's a betting pool on whether tonight's a success or a disaster."

Evie looked at Gwen, her brow furrowing. "There's a betting pool on comedy night? Seriously? Who would do that?"

"Me." Her sister shrugged. "I'm running it. Do you want in?"

"Yes, because it's going to be a huge success."

"I don't really know how odds work and all that, but except for a couple other people, you're pretty much alone in that opinion, so if it's a huge success, you'll win big, I guess."

"Who's defining success? What's the criteria?"

Gwen frowned. "I don't know. Maybe we'll have a family vote. You sure know how to take the fun out of being a rookie bookie. Ha! That rhymes. Maybe I should get a time slot tonight."

"What are you even doing here? Don't you have a book to write?"

"I'm not missing this." Gwen grinned and then made her way back to the table they'd reserved for the family because it seemed like nobody wanted to miss it.

They were even paying one of the neighborhood teens to hang out with Jack and Eli—despite Jack's protests that he was old enough to watch his brother—so Ellen could attend. Laura was a big fan of comedy, so they were having a girl's night of sorts. And Case and Gwen were sitting with them. They'd saved a couple of chairs, too, because Molly was also there, which meant there were plenty of hands on deck and they could take turns sitting down for a while.

Evie checked the sign-up sheet they'd put on the end of the bar, and was pleased to see there were already a few names on the list. She had no idea if they'd be funny, but at least her event wouldn't be met with crickets.

Once she was sure everything would be ready, she grabbed a glass of water and went behind the bar to visit with Lane. It had been a week and a half since she spent the night at his place, and they hadn't been alone since. And while they'd made love several times before she'd left on Sunday— barely beating Laura and her mother home from their trip—it was going to take a lot more than one night and half a day for her to get her fill of him. If that was even possible.

"Did you know Gwen has a betting pool on whether tonight is a success or a disaster?"

He chuckled. "Yup. Already put my money in."

"Seriously?" She narrowed her eyes. "You think it's going to be a disaster, don't you?"

"I put my money on it being a success," he said. She must have shown her surprise because he laughed and moved close enough to put his hand on her hip. Hopefully the bar hid the gesture so her nosy family couldn't see it. "I don't love the idea of open mic nights, but of course I bet on you."

She wanted to kiss him. She couldn't, but she really wanted to.

"Don't look at me like that," he warned, throwing her words back at her. "Not unless you mean it."

"If we were anywhere else, I'd mean it."

He snorted. "Tell me about it. I've actually considered asking Irish if he'll rent me that camper he's got parked out back."

Evie laughed. "I'm almost ready to agree that's a good idea if it means a little privacy."

He turned to face her, leaning his back against the bar and crossing his arms. "You could just come to my house, you know. We're adults."

"You know if Laura or my mom finds out we've been fooling around, on top of this—" She pointed to her very noticeable baby bump. "They'll be planning our wedding."

The look he gave her made her heart stop and she held her breath because it sure looked as if he wanted to say *let's do it* and that couldn't happen. *Please don't say it.*

Things were good. Peaceful. They were not only getting along, but enjoying each other's company. Now was not the time to rock the boat. Not by bringing their family's opinions and expectations into the mix. And certainly not by trying to define what they were doing and where they may or may not be going with it.

"Maybe I can convince Mom and Ellen and to go on a cruise or something," he finally said, and her breezy laugh came partly from relief.

"Hey, Evie." Irish's deep voice had no trouble carrying, even when the taproom was busy. "You want to introduce our first comic?"

She thought *comic* might be a stretch, but she made her way to the table they'd set in front of the glass wall. They all liked the backdrop of the brewing paraphernalia David Sutton had collected over the years, though Evie always had to fight the glare when taking photos. After testing the microphone, she called up the first name on the list.

He got a few laughs, which set a good tone for the evening. The beer flowed, the microphone only cut out twice and everybody was having a good enough time so they even managed laughs and applause for those who weren't as funny as they thought.

"Okay, next on the sign-up sheet is…" Evie paused in her announcement, looking back at the bar. "Molly?"

"Oh, it's my turn!" After setting a glass of the house lager in front of a customer, Molly stepped out from behind the bar and made her way toward Evie. "I've never done this before."

"You'll do great!" Evie handed her the microphone and stepped out of the way.

"Hello, Stonefield!" The crowd laughed, and Evie shook her head as she looked for a good angle to get a few pictures of Molly's act. They were an easy crowd tonight, either thankful to have something to do on a Thursday night or slightly inebriated. Or both.

As Molly launched into a hilarious rant about how hard it was to grow up in a funeral home, Evie went back to the bar. Mallory had done a sweep of the tables before Molly started so they'd all be free to enjoy her jokes, so Evie was free to spend a few more minutes with Lane.

That's how it was now. When they'd first opened the taproom, Evie had spent as much time as possible circulating around the room and only went to the bar when customers asked for more beer. Now she preferred to linger at the bar, and resented when the customers pulled her away from Lane.

"Most kids have sleepovers," Molly was saying. "Do you know how hard it is to get people to sleep in your house when there are dead bodies in the basement?"

Over the roar of laughter, she heard Lane—who'd just taken a sip of coffee—cough and looked to make sure he wasn't choking. He shook his head. "I'm glad her parents are here tonight."

Molly was on a roll now.

"Mom said I should find myself a nice doctor to settle down with, but wouldn't dating a doctor be a conflict of interest?" She paused for the ripple of laughter. "Or maybe it's actually insider trading. And can you imagine the conversation when he came home from work?"

She paused for effect, and Evie was impressed by her timing. Clearly Molly had been practicing in a mirror. Or maybe it was just raw, natural talent.

"How was your day, honey?" Molly said in a high voice, before switching to a deeper male tone. "Good. Didn't lose a single patient today."

"Oh, that's too bad," she finished in the high voice, and then she had to wait for the laughter to subside. "That's my time, everybody. I'm Molly Cyrs. Thank you and good night!"

Once the deafening applause subsided, Lane leaned close to Evie. "Was there a time limit?"

"No. She probably saw it on TV." She watched Molly making her way back to the bar, and it was slow going because everybody wanted to stop her and tell her how much they'd enjoyed her jokes. "I always knew Molly was funny, but I didn't know she was like...stand-up comedian kind of funny."

"I think if we lived in a city, she'd be doing stand-up in the clubs."

She sighed. "One of the drawbacks of living in a town like this. Maybe that was her true calling and she'll never get a chance to try it."

When his jaw tightened, Evie knew she'd touched a nerve. And that nerve was him remembering that Evie had left Stonefield and he believed it was because she wanted something bigger and better than the small town had to offer.

"Evie!" Molly stepped up to the bar, her cheeks as flushed as Evie had ever seen them. "Was I good?"

"Good? Honey, you were brilliant!" She stood on tiptoe and reached out her arms, intending to hug Molly, but her stomach hit the bar and she realized she couldn't reach her. Laughing, she took Molly's hands and squeezed them instead. "You're so funny!"

"I hope you do this again," Molly said, and Evie was thankful the place was noisy because Lane and Irish probably both groaned.

To her surprise, once the taproom was closed and all of the customers had gone home, both guys confessed they would consider doing it again in the future.

"I have to admit that went well," Irish said.

"Definitely better than I thought," Lane agreed.

Mallory laughed. "Really? Did you forget the knock-knock jokes?"

"To be fair," Ellen said, "the other customers seemed to enjoy playing along with those."

"And we sold a lot of beer," Irish said, and then he smiled. "Those two things might be connected."

Evie jabbed Lane's shoulder with her finger. "Hey! What do you mean it went better than you thought it would? You told me you bet on it being a success."

He laughed. "It was five bucks. I bet on you, but I figured I'd be out the money."

She shook her head, but she couldn't be annoyed with him. He *had* bet on her event, after all. There was also the way his eyes crinkled when he smiled at her, and the way those eyes kept dropping to her mouth.

"This was fun," Case said, hooking his arm around Gwen's waist. "But tomorrow's a workday and that alarm goes off early. I think it's bedtime for us."

"I'm ready for bed, too," Laura said. "You're my ride, Lane."

Dammit, Evie thought as Lane frowned. She'd really been hoping to sneak off with him tonight. At least steal some kisses.

"How did you get here?" he asked his mom.

"Ellen picked me up, so we could both drink. She just has to walk across the yard, and I knew you'd be my designated driver, since you're serving, not drinking."

"I can close up here," Irish said. "Go ahead and get your mom home. And your alarm goes off about the same time Case's does. I get to sleep a lot later than you do."

There was no way to argue with that, so Evie was forced to watch Lane and Laura say goodbye to everybody. She got the same "see you tomorrow" that they all got, though Lane did give her a look that let her know he wasn't any happier about it than she was.

Irish's camper wasn't sounding so bad now.

Even though he'd only worked half a day with the tree service, thanks to the good group of guys they had working for them, Lane was exhausted by the time he left the brewing cellar. He'd handled the cleaning alone, since Irish had promised the boys they'd carve pumpkins and it wasn't always easy to find time for things like that. With the boys in school during the day and the taproom open Thursday through Sunday evenings, Tuesday after school was like their weekend.

He'd also been up late texting back and forth with Evie because, no matter how early his alarm went off, he hated ending a conversation with her. There were a lot of text messages and a few phone calls here and there, since it was the only way they really got a chance to communicate privately, but it wasn't the same as actually spending time with her.

He heard the boys laughing and followed the sound to the sawhorses Irish had set up in the back of the yard, where it didn't really matter how much of a mess was made.

They were still in the process of scooping out the pumpkins and it was immediately obvious that Irish had chosen the location well because there was stringy orange stuff everywhere. When Irish saw him coming across the grass, he was visibly relieved and Lane knew he wasn't going to be going home anytime soon.

"Look how big our pumpkins are," Eli said. "Mine's going to have a funny face."

"I'm making mine scary," Jack told him.

"This would be a lot faster if we didn't have to save the seeds," Irish said, nodding toward the large bowl at the end of the sawhorse.

"Yeah." Lane nodded. "But roasted and salted? Worth the effort."

"Especially if it's not your effort," Irish muttered, and Lane laughed.

Shoving his hands in his pockets, he watched them for a few minutes. He'd probably hang out and help them with the carving part because it involved knives, but he didn't have a lot of interest in goop all over his hands.

"So how are things going with—" At the last second, Irish froze. He looked at each of the boys, as though just realizing they were not only listening, but might repeat anything they heard. "The lawn mower. How are things going with the lawn mower?"

"The *lawn mower*?" That was the best Irish could do?

"What's wrong with the lawn mower?" Jack asked, frowning.

Lane knew that Jack was allowed to use the lawn mower now with supervision, so he was going to take this potential problem with his new responsibility very seriously. And since Irish had put himself in this spot, Lane was going to enjoy watching him get himself out of it.

"Irish, is the lawn mower broken?" Jack asked again when he didn't get an answer.

"Not ours," Irish said. "Lane's lawn mower is giving him problems."

"What's the matter with it?" Eli asked, looking up from the pile of pumpkin guts he was sorting.

Lane wasn't the one who'd chosen to turn his lawn mower into the substitute for Evie in this conversation, but it looked like he was stuck with it.

"It's not running smoothly," he finally said. "And it sputters a lot."

Jack's frown intensified. "Maybe you don't have enough spark."

Lane glared at Irish, who was trying to stifle a sudden and highly suspicious cough. He wanted to put an end to this nonsense, but he could see that Jack was trying to be "one of the guys" by sharing the little bit of mechanical knowledge he was picking up.

"I don't think spark is the problem," he said.

"Probably bad gas, then," Jack said, and Irish coughed again.

Lane chuckled. "Bad gas could definitely be why my lawn mower is sputtering."

Satisfied that they'd done a good job of troubleshooting, Jack turned his attention back to scooping out his pumpkin.

Surrendering to the inevitable, Lane stuck his hands in the goop and helped pull out the seeds. He knew from past Halloweens that they'd roast the seeds, but they wouldn't save the rest. Ellen bought her own pumpkins for baking because none of her recipes called for boys' hands all over her ingredients.

While he separated the seeds, he thought about his so-called lawn mower problem. The issue he and Evie were facing right now was that they really seemed to be on a path to being more than friends— or friends with benefits, even—but they didn't get enough alone time to work on their relationship. He'd love to get her out of town for a weekend, but both of them being gone at the same time wouldn't go unnoticed. Especially since they'd have to bring the entire family in to ensure the taproom would be covered.

"You mind overseeing the rest of this?" Irish asked once they'd done most of the cutting. "It's my night to cook and I didn't realize it was getting so late."

"Sure. There's not much left to do anyway." Clean up the edges of the cuts a little, test them with the battery-operated candles Mallory had bought and make sure the tops fit. Then they'd set them on the porch for everybody to admire. In other words, the fun stuff. "What are you making?"

"Beef stew. Mallory and her mom baked some

sourdough loaves and there's nothing better than beef stew with fresh bread. You staying?"

"I just had dinner here last night, with the meeting and all. I don't want to wear out my welcome."

"Trust me—there's more than enough."

Lane wanted to say yes—he was a sucker for homemade sourdough—but he hesitated. Having dinner with the Sutton family meant having dinner with Evie and he wasn't sure how he felt about that.

He and his mom had planned to reheat leftovers for supper tonight, and Irish's beef stew definitely sounded a lot more appetizing. His stomach rumbled just thinking about it. But he and Evie were keeping secrets from them and it wasn't easy for him to hide things from people he cared about. Okay, so it probably wasn't the best kept of secrets, but as far as he knew, neither of their mothers had caught on to the fact they'd been rekindling the flame, so to speak. And he knew Evie wanted to keep it that way.

"You know you want to," Irish said when Lane didn't respond right away. "So just say yes."

Lane tipped his head toward the boys. "That lawn mower, though. The sputtering and all."

"Hey, even when the lawn mower won't run, the grass keeps on growing."

Lane frowned. "I... I don't know what that means."

"I don't, either." Irish shook his head. "I was going for pointing out that no matter what's going on, a man's gotta eat."

"Now that, I understand. I'm in."

He sent a text to his mom letting her know he wouldn't be joining her for leftovers and took the plastic knife Eli handed him. By the time he and the boys had set the illuminated jack-o'-lanterns on the porch steps and done as much cleaning up as they could manage without dragging the hose out, he was cold and starving. Walking into the warm Sutton house, he closed his eyes and inhaled the aroma of warm bread as the boys took off toward the kitchen.

A floorboard creaking made him open his eyes, and he saw Evie coming down the stairs. Her face lit up when she saw him, and that warmed him even more than coming inside had. He toed off his boots in time to meet her at the bottom of the stairs.

After glancing around to make sure they were alone, he cupped her cheek in his palm and kissed her. Not nearly as deeply or as long as he wanted to, but maybe it would be enough to get him through another night of wanting her.

"It sounds like everybody's in the kitchen and dining room," he said in a low voice. "Maybe we could sneak upstairs for a few minutes and nobody would notice."

"Evie! Dinner's ready," Ellen called from the kitchen.

Lane groaned, dropping his head. "Or maybe not."

"Your hands are really cold anyway," she said. "But we'll figure something out soon."

"*Very* soon." He wiped a smear of pumpkin from her cheek. "I'm going to go to the bathroom and clean up and then I'll be in."

Her eyes widened. "You're eating with us?"

"Irish invited me. Is that okay?"

"Of course. I'll see you in the dining room."

When he joined the family, the chairs on either side of Evie were taken, so he sat across from her. He wouldn't be able hook his leg around hers in a secret substitute for holding hands, but at least he'd be able to see her.

There was a lot of chatter while they ate. The boys were excited about Halloween, and there was a talk about trick-or-treating and which friends they wanted to go with. Evie was quiet, mostly, since Jack and Eli were dominating the conversation, but she kept smiling at him across the table. He ached to be alone with her, and his mind spent a lot more time thinking about that than it did the route the boys wanted to map out to maximize their candy haul.

"There's only a week and a half left until the Halloween party," Ellen said once the boys ran out of steam. "Do you all have your costumes figured out?"

Lane grimaced. He wasn't big into the costume idea, but he knew he'd never hear the end of it if he opted out. His mother kept coming up with out-landish ideas that would require a lot more time and money than he wanted to put into a costume, and he'd been keeping her at bay by pointing out he'd be tending bar all night. That was going to be hard to do with tentacles or a suit of armor made of cardboard and aluminum foil.

He'd asked Evie several times what she was going to be, but she refused to tell him. They were all supposed to be surprises. He'd even tried pointing out that it wasn't fair that everybody else would be planning in pairs, but she'd caught on to that quickly.

I'm not choosing or making your costume for you, Lane.

He'd think of something. Maybe he'd throw on one of the Patriots jerseys he had kicking around, put a black stripe under each eye and call himself a quarterback.

Maybe he could get Evie into the brewing cellar, he thought. He could tell them he'd been thinking about doing a series of photos of the equipment downstairs—a peek behind the curtain, so to speak—and since they'd just done a thorough cleaning, it would be a good time for her to take pictures.

That could work. Not that he was going to make love to her in a cellar, no matter how clean it was, but they could be alone. Maybe make out a little.

"Oh, Evie," Mallory said before he could open his mouth and put the plan in motion. "I've got a backlog of things in the shop room upstairs that we need to price and some of them need photos so they can go online. Some of it's seasonal, like for Thanksgiving and Christmas, so I really need to catch up. Can you give me a hand after dinner? Irish will run herd on the boys so we can get through it."

Damn. He wouldn't be making out with Evie tonight, though he was going to file that plan away for another time. It would have worked, too.

Chapter Thirteen

At last night's meeting of the selectmen, the chief of police stated that everybody in this town knows where High Street is and the best course of action is to not bother replacing the sign. When the fire chief countered with an argument that all streets have to be clearly identified for 9-1-1 purposes, the police chief asked every single member of the fire and police departments who were present if they know where High Street is. When they all affirmed they did, the fire chief said that wasn't the point.

The issue of the sign was tabled temporarily after the police chief made an inappro-

priate hand gesture, to which the fire chief took offense. We reached out to Chelsea Grey, owner of the Perkin' Up Café, to ask if the two chiefs met for their customary morning coffee, but she declined to comment.
—Stonefield Gazette *Facebook Page*

Evie walked into the taproom an hour before they'd be opening the doors to put a few final touches on the Halloween party decorations. They'd also agreed the family should all arrive in advance so they could admire each other's costumes and take some pictures.

Mallory, who was dressed in a sparkly gold dress that hugged her curves and had probably made Irish's jaw drop, saw her and frowned. "Really, Evie?"

"What?" She looked down at the black tunic she was wearing over black leggings. She'd borrowed flat-soled black leather boots from Gwen, and she had a cat-ear headband on. She'd even put a pink dot on her nose and drawn on whiskers. "I'm a cat."

"I can see that you're a cat. What about what you're wearing required you to be gone for two hours for a costume emergency?"

Evie's cheeks warmed, probably turning a shade of pink that matched her nose. The costume emergency had been a text message from Lane.

Case needs extra time for his costume, so we're

heading home before lunch. Mom has a meeting of some club or another until two-thirty. I'm alone.

He hadn't been alone for long, and Evie's muscles were still deliciously languid from the orgasms he'd given her. She wasn't, however, going to share that information with her sister. "I needed pink for my nose."

Mallory smirked. "Yeah, Mom hasn't worn makeup in a while, but I know her favorite shade of pink when I see it."

"What are *you* supposed to be?"

Mallory stepped closer and pointed to the small name tag she'd pinned to the gold dress. "I'm a Bond girl."

"What does that mean?"

"Irish!" A few seconds after she yelled, Irish stepped out of the kitchen.

Or at least she thought it was Irish. The man in the tuxedo with the slicked-down hair bore little resemblance to the cowboy her sister had married. "Ooooh, James Bond. And a Bond girl. That's cute."

The door opened and her nephews rushed in, followed by Ellen. Case and Gwen were right behind her.

"I'm a superhero," Eli yelled, throwing up his arms and almost tossing the shield with the star in the center.

"And I'm a supervillain," Jack said, holding up

his hand so they could see he was wearing some kind of glove with fake gemstones in the knuckles.

Evie had no idea who they were. She was going to have to start paying attention to what the kids were into, she realized. Not quite yet, because it would be a few years before her child joined any fandoms, but at some point her life was going to revolve around books and movies and games for tots.

Her mother was wearing a full-skirted dress that looked like it was from the fifties, along with a wig of bright red curls. It took Evie a second to recall the name Lucille Ball, from the *I Love Lucy* reruns her parents had watched together sometimes, but she had to admit her mom had done a good job on her costume.

Case and Gwen would be hard to beat, though. Gwen was wearing jeans, hiking boots, a red-and-black-checked flannel shirt and a knit cap. And she had a plastic ax, completing the lumberjack look. Case was wearing a brown Henley tucked into brown pants, and they'd attached sticks with green paper leaves to his torso. His knit cap was also covered in fake leaves, making him a perfect tree.

"Is Lane here yet?" Ellen asked, looking around the room. "He's bringing Laura with him."

"They should be here any minute," Evie said, and when they all looked at her, she realized she shouldn't know that. But she did because Lane had sent her a text message letting her know he was on his way, and also letting her know he was looking forward to seeing her costume. "I mean, he knew what time we were coming over here and Laura hates to be late."

As if on cue, the door opened and Lane walked in with his mom. Evie took a moment to register that Laura was wearing a costume almost identical to Ellen's, and then she saw Lane.

"No," she said, and then she winced because she hadn't meant to say it out loud.

He was wearing a brown long-sleeved T-shirt and brown pants, like Case, but he wasn't a tree. He was wearing a brown ball cap with what looked like furry German shepherd ears attached to it, and there was a smudge of black on his nose.

He was a dog.

Eli laughed. "That's funny. Aunt Evie's a cat and Lane's a dog."

"I get it," Jack said. "Because they fight like cats and dogs!"

Gwen laughed. "Sorry. But it's true."

It really wasn't. Not anymore. But Evie wasn't about to correct her in front of everybody, so she just smiled.

"Did you plan this?" Laura asked.

"No," Evie and Lane said at the same time.

"Aunt Evie looks like a cat who's going to have a *lot* of kittens," Eli said, and they all laughed, especially when Lane made a face of mock horror.

Evie rolled her eyes, and then made her way to the bar, where she snagged a piece of candy from the bowl they had for any kids who showed up at the door. Her sisters joined her, talking about whether they'd brought enough napkins down from the upstairs storage area.

She leaned close to Mallory. "Why are Mom and Laura dressed as twin Lucille Balls? I thought they were doing something together."

Her sister snorted. "Because they decided that Lucy and Ethel would be the best best-friends' costumes ever and then they not only argued for two weeks about who had to be Ethel, but they both spent those two weeks making Lucy costumes."

"They're having fun. That's all that really matters, I guess."

"For now." Mallory pointed at the best costume voting box. "It's all fun and games until one Lucy wins best costume and the other Lucy doesn't."

Evie unwrapped another bite-size candy bar and popped it in her mouth, dropping the wrapper into the small pile she was collecting.

"Stop eating the candy," Gwen told her, sliding the bowl away from her. "It's for the kids."

"There won't be many kids. People aren't going to dress their kids up to bring them here and then do it all over again in three days." She snagged the bowl and slid it back.

"It's going to be a long night," Mallory said, picking up the bowl and moving it out of her reach. "If you pound sugar the whole time, that baby's going to have you up all night."

"I swear it's like having three mothers." Evie snorted. "And people wonder why I left Stonefield."

"You're being so ridiculous right now," Gwen told her in that tone that irked her to no end.

"Really? You and Mal are super tight and older than me, so all three of you would tell me what to do and hover over me and yeah, three moms."

"You're exaggerating."

"I'm not."

The discussion ended when the door opened and Molly walked through, wearing a cheerleader uniform that Evie was pretty sure was her *actual* uniform from high school. After shaking shiny gold pom-poms, Molly kicked one long leg up in the air, and then jumped up and down. "Happy Halloween party night!"

Mallory shook her head, but she was grinning. "She's going to make *great* tips tonight."

The taproom was absolute chaos. The best kind of chaos, Lane knew, because crowds and laughter meant money in the bank, but they were having trouble keeping up and he was pretty sure sweat had washed away his dog nose an hour into the party.

On the positive side, it kept him from having too much free time to obsess about the comment he'd overheard Evie make to her sisters before the taproom opened.

And people wonder why I left Stonefield.

He knew she'd only been pushing their buttons—or

at least he hoped that's all it was—but it had thrown him off for a while. Every time he started to feel even a little secure in his relationship with Evie, she would say something that reminded him of all the times she'd left and brought him right back to the divorce.

He didn't want to think about that anymore, but he didn't know how to stop.

Irish stepped up next to him, tugging at the bow tie that had been strangling him all night. "I don't think it's fair that I couldn't be a cowboy but Case gets to be a tree."

"I'm not actually a tree in real life," Case pointed out. He was sitting on a barstool, nursing a beer and trying to stay out of the way. He'd already lost some of his branches to customers squeezing by him, and he was looking ragged.

"It might be close enough to disqualify you from Best Couple's Costume," Lane said. He didn't really care, but he was always up for giving his cousin a hard time.

Case snorted. "I dare you to go tell Gwen that."

"I'll pass." He was no fool.

Movement caught his eye and Lane looked over Case's shoulder to see Evie approaching. She had to be hot as hell in that long shirt and tights, but whatever she'd used to draw on her whiskers had more staying power than the smudge he'd put on his nose. And he had to admit he liked the way the fabric hugged her stomach, showing off a baby bump that was quickly becoming more of a baby basketball.

She slid onto the stool next to Case, fighting her way through the branches that were the reason nobody else would sit there, and gave him a tired smile. "What a night, huh?"

"Will you bite my head off if I tell you to take a break?" he asked, knowing how much she hated being told what to do.

"That's what I'm doing right now. I'm going to sit here and ignore the customers while you pour these drinks." She slid the beer order across the bar and then cast a sad glance at the empty candy bowl. "Mallory said we should announce the costume winners soon so we can start getting people out of here. Gwen and Molly are counting them right now."

He took his time pouring the beer orders, trying to extend her break—such as it was—if only for a couple of minutes. "You're going to need a foot rub after all the walking you've done tonight."

She smiled. "You volunteering?"

Lane was aware of Case and Irish being very interested in straightening coasters, trying to look as if they weren't paying attention. "Sure. That's my kid you're lugging around, so it's only fair."

He could tell by her expression that she knew what he'd done. He'd managed to explain away a reason to touch her without raising too many eyebrows. What she might not know was that it wasn't necessary. The two men within earshot knew he'd never stopped loving her and they also knew he had no willpower. He and Evie were probably the worst-kept secret in town.

"Are you sticking around tonight?" she asked. "To help clean up, I mean."

"Yeah. In the chaos, you probably didn't notice her leave, but my mother's already asleep on your couch, and your mother is half-asleep in the recliner. When Mallory checked on the boys, they were almost asleep on the floor watching a movie and she said we're just going to leave them all there."

"Can I have your attention, everybody?" Gwen had the microphone, and the customers quieted. "It's time to announce the winners!"

Evie gave Lane a smile and slid off the stool, barely managing to avoid getting slapped in the face by one of Case's branches. After taking the two glasses he set in front of her, she went to deliver them. He watched her walk away, and wasn't surprised when he caught Case and Irish sharing a *yeah, he's got it bad* look.

Lane knew he did, in fact, have it bad.

Nobody was shocked when the winner of the Best Costume was announced as Molly Cyrs. She was wearing a cheerleading uniform and a whole lot of men drinking beer had voted tonight. They'd also emptied the tip bucket a record number of times, and he was pretty sure that was thanks more to her than to his and Irish's bartending.

The Best Couple's Costume was rightly awarded to Han Solo and Princess Leia, who were wearing what looked like very expensive, professional-level costumes. The crowd applauded as Gwen called them up to get their gift card.

"You look amazing," she told them.

"I know," the man said, and laughter rippled through the thinning crowd.

It was twenty minutes after they technically closed before they got the last customer out the door and Irish locked it with visible relief. "We're all sleeping in tomorrow."

The six of them made quick work of cleaning up and closing out the register, until all that was left was running a few stray glasses through the autoclave.

"You guys should go," Evie told the others. "Boomer's probably waiting for you guys so he can go to bed, and I'd bet good money there are two boys who are going to need a boost from Irish to get upstairs. I'll help Lane finish with the glasses and lock up."

Nobody argued, and Lane wondered how much of that was sheer exhaustion and how much was them recognizing Evie looking for a few minutes alone with him. But he didn't really care, as long as they left.

Once they were finally alone, Lane lifted Evie onto a barstool and stood between her legs. "I'm worried you're doing too much, Evie. You were on your feet all night."

She shrugged. "I have to work, though. I can't just hang out in my bed all day, eating bonbons."

"What *are* bonbons, anyway?"

"I don't really know." She laughed. "But they sound decadent, don't they?"

"I'm going to find out what they are and get you some," he promised right before she slid her hands over his shoulders and pulled him in for a kiss.

Would there ever come a time kissing this woman didn't bring a rush of emotion, anticipation and pleasure? He really hoped not.

They kissed until they had to come up for air, and then he rested his forehead against hers. "I've been dying to do that all night."

"Me, too," she whispered. "Let's do the glasses and then we can kiss some more."

"You stay right here," he said. "I'll take care of the glasses."

He finished in the kitchen in record time, and once he was satisfied everything was done, he went back to Evie. She was leaned on the bar now, one hand propping up her head. Lane was glad he hadn't taken any longer because if she fell asleep like that and her hand slipped, she was going to give herself a concussion.

She straightened when he put his hand on her back, and then she leaned against him.

"You need to go in and go to bed," he told her, even though it was the last thing he actually wanted her to do.

"I want to stay out here with you. We're never alone."

"I know, but it was a long night, sweetheart." He couldn't resist one last kiss good-night, though.

Tipping her face up, he lowered his mouth to hers. Her arms wrapped around his waist, and he cradled her head in his hand as he took his time kissing her.

Then his phone chimed.

"Your fault this time," she murmured against his mouth.

With a sigh, he pulled out his phone, certain his mother had woken up and wanted to go home. But the text message was from Irish, and Lane wondered how long it had taken his tech-hating friend to type it out.

Ellen and Laura are tucked into Ellen's bed, snoring. The boys are asleep. And Mallory face-planted on the bed and I think she's sleeping in her dress. The coast is clear if you're looking for a place to give Evie that foot rub you owe her.

He chuckled, and when Evie gave him a questioning look, he showed her the screen.

"I've always liked that guy," she said with a grin. "You know, if your mother's sleeping in my house, there's nobody in *your* house."

As much as the idea of her being in his bed again made his blood heat, he was exhausted, which meant she had to be absolutely drained. "Neither of us is going to get out of bed early enough in the morning to have you back here before the moms are up. What do you think the chances are we can sneak up to your room for a little bit without getting caught?"

She hooked her finger in the neck of his shirt and tugged him closer. "Usually, not good. But tonight? I think we can risk it."

"You should know up front I'm too old to climb out the window if somebody wakes up."

"I bet you'd fit in my closet if I shoved you hard enough, though." She kissed him—hard and fast—and then released his shirt. "Lock up and let's go."

Chapter Fourteen

Don't forget that Sutton's Place Brewery &
Tavern will be hosting another open mic night
tonight, and this time it's poetry! Evie Sut-
ton says anybody can stand up and recite a
poem they wrote, but they're also open to peo-
ple reading a favorite piece of poetry. Lane
Thompson assures us there will be plenty of
beer on tap to help get everybody through
the night.

—Stonefield Gazette *Facebook Page*

"You should have argued harder against this,"
Evie said, shaking her head at Lane.

He gave her a smug look that made her want to

shake one of the growlers of beer and then open it in his face. "Hey, it was your idea. But also, I told you so."

"I thought it would be fun."

"Apparently, you also thought the people who live in this town are poetic."

"I was wrong."

"I should have my mom cross-stitch that on a bar towel."

She laughed because if she didn't, she was either going to cry or yank the microphone out of the current poet's hand and yell at everybody to get out. "I'm taking a break for a few minutes. I need some fresh air."

"Right now?" The citizens of Stonefield had really turned out for poetry night, which was a testament to how little there was to do in their small town, and the place was packed.

"Don't make me use the baby as an excuse." She smiled and gave him a little wave before walking out the door.

She'd only been sitting on the porch of the house, breathing in the chilly night air, for a few minutes when she got a text from Mallory calling her back to the taproom. Groaning, she pushed herself out of the chair and she could hear the excited chatter before she even opened the door.

After spotting Mallory at the end of the bar, Evie went directly to her. "What's going on? And where's Lane?"

"Lane is locking the microphone equipment in the cellar and he said to tell you he'll change the passcode if you try to get it back. And what's going on is that Al recited a limerick that made George throw a buffalo wing at him and then Peggy fainted."

"Peggy fainted because George threw a buffalo wing at Al?"

"I think it was the limerick, actually."

A case of poetry-induced vapors? That was new. "Just how bad was it?"

"Let me just reiterate the fact Peggy fainted." Mallory rolled her eyes. "One of the lines was 'though his tool was quite blunt' and the limerick did not contain the words *hunt*, *runt* or *punt*."

"Shunt?"

"There was nary a *shunt*, nor a *front* nor a *grunt*." Mallory fought a grin and lost. "Except when Frank had to catch Peggy before she hit the floor. Then there was grunting."

"We're deep-sixing poetry night." Evie watched Irish fussing over Peggy as he helped her into a chair. "Fainting seems a little extreme, though."

"It's possible she tried to gasp in outrage and her Spanx fought back." Mallory winced. "Okay, that was a little mean, but she has her arms wrapped around my husband's neck right now and there's no reason to because her ass is firmly in that chair."

Lane came up the stairs and, after making sure the door had closed and locked behind them, joined them in the bar huddle. "No more open mic nights."

Evie frowned at him. "Just because poetry night went a little sideways doesn't—"

"There's buffalo sauce on the glass, Evie. That's not a *little* sideways."

"If you'll excuse me," Mallory said, "I need to go disentangle my husband from Peggy's tentacles."

"Tell her we took care of her bar bill for the night, and offer apologies." Lane gave Mallory a stern look. "And I know how you Sutton women are, so do *not* use any word that rhymes with *blunt*."

Mallory gave him a deceptively sweet smile and walked away, and probably not a moment too soon because Peggy was still clutching Irish and he was shooting them a look that was an obvious cry for help. And judging by the current vibe, their customers found flying buffalo wings and outraged women a lot more entertaining than poetry.

Evie leaned against the bar and waited for Lane to pour refills for the two guys who cared more about the game on the TV over Lane's head than they did about the drama that had unfolded behind them. She was exhausted and looking forward to putting her feet up. Or maybe she'd skip the putting her feet up part and go straight to crawling into her bed.

"You can take another break, you know," Lane told her, having gravitated back to her when the customers were taken care of.

"I'm good."

"Evie, you're obviously tired."

She smiled, shaking her head. "Everybody's tired."

"Everybody's not pregnant."

She covered his hand with hers for a few seconds before pulling it back because they were surrounded by people and most of them were nosy. "We close in an hour. I'll be fine."

"As soon as we close, you should go back to the house. I can handle the cleanup with Irish."

"Lane, you have to get up and go to work in the morning. Stop fussing over me."

He leaned across the bar, bringing his face closer to hers as his mouth curved into a smile that was a little bit sweet but a whole lot of naughty. "But I like fussing over you."

Before she could think of anything to say to *that*, Irish joined them. "That woman has one hell of a grip."

"Is she okay?" Evie asked. Even if Peggy had taken the opportunity to get her hands on Irish—which was understandable, honestly—they needed to make sure she wasn't hurt. Customers tumbling out of chairs and onto the hard floor wasn't great.

"She's okay. Rumor has it she didn't actually pass out, but was being dramatic." Irish tilted his head in the way he had of indicating a shrug. "The source was her husband, so I think she's fine."

"Good." Evie rolled her eyes. "I'll get the glass cleaner and take care of the buffalo sauce."

By the time they closed, Evie was beat and when

Mallory told her to go to bed, she felt bad about it, but she went. There was no opportunity to get Lane alone for a good-night kiss, so she had to settle for a wave and a look that promised her they'd find a way to be alone again soon.

The next morning, Evie waited until the house was quiet to venture downstairs. She adored Jack and Eli, but that window between them waking up and walking out the door for school was pure chaos. *Something to look forward to*, she thought, chuckling to herself as she walked into the kitchen.

Where she stopped short because her mother was sitting at the table, drinking coffee with her notebook open in front of her. "Good morning, honey."

"Morning." Evie went straight to the fridge. "You're not going to the shop today?"

"Later. Laura and I are taking a little road trip to pick up some cast-iron pans I bought on Facebook. Some cleaning and seasoning and I'll triple my money, at least."

Evie wrinkled her nose. Though she knew rescuing neglected cast iron was money in the bank, she'd always hated the smell of the season process.

"I heard a rumor there was a food fight in the taproom last night," her mom said, and Evie didn't have to see her face to know she wasn't happy about it.

She pulled out the juice and a bowl of cut-up fruit before closing the door with her foot. "Like most of the gossip in this town, that rumor is not true."

"So nobody threw food?"

Evie sat at the table, not meeting her mother's eyes. "George did throw a buffalo wing at Al."

"You just told me the rumor isn't true."

"I told you the rumor there was a food fight isn't true. There was no food fight." Evie pushed chunks of honeydew aside in the bowl, looking for cantaloupe. "Nobody threw food *back* at George. *Then* it would have been a food fight."

"Don't be fresh."

"What are you working on?" Evie asked, nodding at the notebook. It was time to change the subject.

"I'm working on Thanksgiving plans."

"Thanksgiving's not for two weeks." Evie snorted. "And planning it won't take long. Just write *same as last year* on a sticky note and put it on the fridge."

"Sitting ten people is going to require some planning." She frowned. "I really don't want to put Jack and Eli at a card table."

"Ten?" She didn't even have to ask who the additional two were.

The idea of Lane being in the house with her entire family for the better part of a day made Evie's stomach hurt. They were in such a good place, but she knew that was partly because there was no pressure on it. The only time they were really seen together was at work, and when they were in the taproom, they were focused on the job. Mostly. Sure, there were looks and touches and occasional stolen moments, but that was different than the two of them being together under the family's microscope for an entire day.

"Aren't Laura and Lane doing their own thing?" she asked, even though she already knew the answer.

"That's a lot of work for two people, so I invited them to join us. We always have more than enough food."

"Thanksgiving is about family."

Ellen gave her a stern mom look. "You're saying that because things between you and Lane are complicated and I understand that, but please don't diminish my friendship with Laura. She's like family to me and there's no reason she and her son need to be alone for the holiday."

Evie hoped her mother didn't know just how complicated things really were between her and Lane right now. "I'm sorry, Mom. You're right."

"Family means a lot of things."

"It does." She chuckled. "Besides, Laura's going to be your grandchild's grandmother."

Ellen laughed. "That's true. And when it comes down to it, Lane *is* your sister's fiancé's cousin."

And the father of her baby, Evie thought, settling her hand on her stomach. One couldn't get more family than that.

Family.

It was a word that had always brought to mind her sisters. Her parents. Memories of her dad. But now when she heard the word, the first face that popped into her mind was Lane's and that terrified her. Something had shifted in their relationship—something that made it easy to imagine her and Lane together, raising their baby and maybe having more. Falling asleep with him and waking up next to him. Sharing a life together.

But, no matter what her heart said, she couldn't trust it. They'd been down this road too many times for her to not know that at some point along the journey, there would be a fork and they'd get pulled in different directions. Or they'd just run off the road.

She wanted it, though. Whether it was a good idea or not, the heart wants what it wants, and her heart wanted Lane.

Lane didn't usually mind the Monday night brewery meetings because they included a free meal, but tonight sitting across the table from Evie was killing him.

In the week and a half since the poetry night disaster, they'd only been alone twice. This dance they were doing—being together, but hiding it from everybody in their lives—was getting old. She was so worried about them having opinions and expectations but, dammit, what about *his* expectations?

As far as he was concerned, they'd played this game long enough. They weren't doing anything wrong and, as far as he could tell, not a single person in the room would be surprised or upset by the news he and Evie were seeing each other.

By the time Mallory was finished with her accounting report, he was starting to think he should have skipped this meeting. He could have told them he had a headache or something. He'd wrenched his shoulder at work—not bad, but enough so there was a nagging ache in it. Between that and his growing dissatisfaction with the state of affairs between him and Evie, he wasn't in the mood for it.

"Okay, on to events," Evie said, and Lane heard Irish sigh.

"I was thinking we could do a toy drive before Christmas," she continued. "Bring a toy, get one free pour or something like that."

Ellen stopped tapping her pen on her notebook. "I like that idea."

"And then there's New Year's Eve, of course."

Irish cleared his throat, looking uncomfortable. "We should talk about the events."

"We are," Evie said. "That's literally what we're doing right now."

"I mean we should talk about how much time, energy and occasionally money we're putting into doing them," he clarified. "Of course I'm on board for a toy drive, but overall I'd like to see us pull back a little."

"It's good marketing, though. I can only post so many pictures of a glass of beer on a bar."

Irish nodded, but Lane could tell the man had

more he wanted to say. But he looked uncomfortable enough to let it go, so Lane jumped in on his behalf. "We do need to dial them back a little, though. Between the tree service and the thrift shop and your pregnancy, there's a lot on everybody's plates and we need to keep the focus on the brewing and the taproom."

Evie's mouth tightened, and he knew he'd pushed that annoyance button only he seemed to push. "Sure, Lane, because *hey, come watch people sit and drink beer* is a great marketing caption."

"It's literally what a taproom is for," he shot back.

"I get what you're saying, Evie," Mallory said, giving Lane a quick look meant to silence him. "But we need to be more selective and space the events out a little. And maybe think smaller."

"Maybe the brewery and taproom aren't exciting enough for you, Evie," Gwen said, in a sharper tone than Mal had used. "But they're what we do and what we need to focus our energy on, whether you find it boring or not."

Lane knew Gwen's attitude was going to set Evie off and, sure enough, the two sisters started bickering, with Mallory trying to mediate. He tuned them out, though, because regardless of whether or not she'd said them just to annoy Evie, Gwen's words had gotten under his skin.

As if on cue, the pang had come—the reminder of the past that shook his confidence about him and Evie getting it right this time.

Maybe the brewery and taproom aren't exciting enough for you.

Evie was doing whatever she could to not get bored with Sutton's Place Brewery & Tavern and since she hadn't been there all that long, it wasn't a good sign. Stonefield wasn't the most exciting town to live in. She'd never liked working in the thrift shop. Serving customers in the taproom played to her strengths—she was fun and friendly and loved talking to different people—so if that wasn't enough for her without open mic nights and parties and karaoke, she was going to want to move on.

By the time the baby was born, Evie was going to be itching to get in that Jeep and leave them all in her rearview mirror and he couldn't let himself forget that.

"*We*, Gwen?" Evie snorted. "How many hours have *you* spent waiting tables in the taproom?"

"I do what I can, and it's still a family business. And who do you think is going to be picking up the slack while you're on maternity leave?"

"Molly."

"Girls." Ellen said the word like a command, and everybody fell silent. "The holidays are coming up. We have a baby to prepare for. I say we do the toy drive, but table anything else for a while. As for New Year's Eve, I'm not sure I want people here drinking until midnight and, Evie, you'll be a couple of weeks away from having that baby, and that's *if* you go to your due date. We can talk about it, but not tonight."

They all nodded, but she wasn't done. "I also think we can do these meetings every other week, instead of every week. Maybe even once a month, eventually. We've got a handle on things now. And they're going to be potluck in the future because I'm sick of cooking a big meal every week on my day off."

Eyes were wide all around the table, and Lane knew he wasn't the only one in an off mood today. And he was ready to be done with this. "I think we should call it a night. With Thanksgiving this week and our regular closed nights, we've got over a week off from the taproom and we should take the mental rest as well as the physical. Irish and I will need to be in the cellar a bit, of course, but let's all take a break."

"I agree," Ellen said, and that was the end of it.

While everybody shuffled notebooks and moved around, Lane walked out to the front porch. He wouldn't leave without saying goodbye, but he needed some fresh air.

A few minutes later, he heard the screen door open and Evie joined him at the railing. "Hey, are you okay?"

"Yeah. Warm in there."

She chuckled. "You and Case work outside year-round, so you always think it's too warm in the house once the heat's on."

He nodded, but he couldn't come up with the right words to continue the small talk. Not now.

"Gwen wasn't right, you know." She sighed, bending to lean on the porch railing. "About me trying to make the taproom more exciting because I'm bored."

Lane wasn't sure what to say to that. Her sisters knew her better than anybody, and the words had certainly rung true. Evie didn't stay put in one place for very long, and she liked adventures. Opening the brewery had certainly qualified, but the day-to-day work, not so much.

"Planning events makes me feel like I'm doing something besides waiting tables," she said, and there was something in her voice that made him turn to her. "You all have other jobs, Lane. You all work *so* hard, and this and carrying drinks is all I do. I don't feel like it's enough most of the time. But when I plan something and it brings customers in and they have a great time, I feel like I did my part—that I'm earning my keep."

"The customers love you, Evie, and you're a great server. You don't have to throw parties for them, too. You have a way with people—you remember them and you make them feel like they *belong*, and Irish and I can't do that. We can make small talk and rehash ball games and that, but it's not the same. Every single person who walks through those doors—and that includes us—missed you while you were away."

She sniffed and swiped at her eyes. "It just doesn't feel like enough sometimes."

"It's enough." He took her chin between his fingers and brought her gaze up to his. "You bring something to Sutton's Place that nobody else does, not even your mom or your sisters. You make the customers so welcome, they almost feel like family, and *that* was David's dream. He and I talked about this for years, and that's what he wanted this place to be—the heart of the community. That's what you bring, Evie, so don't ever feel like you're not doing enough."

When her face crumpled, he pulled her into his arms and pressed a kiss to the top of his head. He didn't really care if anybody came looking for her or happened to glance out a window and caught them embracing. He held her until she took a deep, steadying breath and lifted her head.

"Thank you, Lane."

Then she burrowed against him again and he rested his cheek on her head. Maybe he'd been reading it all wrong. Maybe it was true that, rather than wishing she could leave, she was trying to make a place for herself that felt truly hers.

But he couldn't help fearing it wouldn't be enough.

Chapter Fifteen

*Happy Thanksgiving, Stonefield! We hope you
all have a wonderful day with your families.
A reader reported that yesterday, on her way
to the Perkin' Up Café for a much needed
caffeine boost, she spotted them readying the
wreaths at the town garage. Get ready to see
some festivity hanging from the lamp posts by
the end of next week!*

—Stonefield Gazette *Facebook Page*

They managed to get all ten of them around the
dining room table without leaving Jack and Eli to
eat in the kitchen, but it was a tight fit and there
wasn't a lot of elbow room. Of course Evie had been

seated next to Lane. She didn't mind bumping arms with him or the heat of his leg pressed against hers, but being so close to him was a constant reminder it had been at least a week since they'd bumped anything else.

So her plan for getting through Thanksgiving dinner was filling herself so full of food, she wouldn't even want to think about having sex with Lane.

Luckily, between the three households, they'd prepared enough food to put the entire neighborhood in a food coma. And having a little break from each other, as well as having a few more days of vacation left, had improved everybody's moods. They were talking about everything *but* the brewery, and they all seemed happy with that.

"Are you going to make our baby hate vegetables?" Lane asked in a low voice, leaning toward her in a way that made her shiver.

She looked down at her plate, which was loaded with turkey, mashed potatoes drowning in gravy and a whole lot of cranberry sauce. "There wasn't any room left for vegetables. And cranberries are a fruit."

He chuckled and nudged the bowl of squash toward her. She wrinkled her nose and turned to Jack, who was on the other side of her. "Want some squash?"

"Ew. No. The green beans are good, though."

When they were about halfway through the meal,

Ellen pushed back from the table. "I should start putting the pies in the oven."

"I'll help," Gwen said.

Thinking about the pies made Evie regret the amount of mashed potatoes she'd put on her plate, but she was going to make it work. Maybe once she could move again, she'd go for a walk around the block in between dinner and pie time. They usually served the pie about two hours after the meal so even at her slow pace, she could probably make it in time.

"Evie, have you thought about what you're going to do after the baby's born?" Laura asked, seemingly out of nowhere.

Evie froze with her fork halfway to her mouth. "What do you mean?"

"I assume you'll keep working at the taproom, but have you thought about where you'll live?"

She didn't really understand the question. "I... live here."

"Sure, you're staying here, but it's a full house. And with the thrift store during the day and watching the boys most nights, Ellen's got her hands full."

Evie lowered the uneaten forkful of cranberry sauce back to the plate. Where was this coming from? Was this something her mother had been talking to her best friend about? Maybe her mom thought having Evie and a newborn in the house would be too much and she didn't know how to tell her.

"Our house, on the other hand, has all kinds of room." Laura gave her a warm smile. "And I work from home, so I'm always available. I could even put a crib in the office."

"Are you…" Evie stopped, turning to Lane for help, but he was staring at his mother and didn't seem to notice her confusion. "Are you offering to babysit?"

Laura laughed. "No. Well, yes, actually. I'd take care of the baby when you both need to be at the brewery, of course. What I'm saying is that you and the baby should move in with us."

"Mom." Lane's voice was low, like a warning.

"What? If you think about it, it makes sense. I'll be there to help and you two…it's not really a secret you've become close again. It's the perfect situation."

Evie wasn't sure if Lane responded to that or not because there was nothing but a buzzing in her head.

This. This was what she hadn't wanted—their mothers interfering in their fragile relationship. And she'd never even considered the possibility having an infant in the house would be overwhelming for her mom and the rest of the family.

"I don't know," she said, not knowing what else she *could* say. This was neither the time nor the place to get into it with Laura about boundaries. "I don't know what I'm doing after the baby's born."

"We have plenty of room," she heard Mallory say. "And plenty of hands to take care of the baby."

Of course Mallory would take her side, but Mallory had two rambunctious young boys. She juggled working at the thrift store and the taproom, and she was a newlywed on top of it.

And Lane was just staring at his mother, his jaw clenched so hard, Evie wondered if he'd have to pry it open with the fork he was strangling. She guessed it was too much to ask for him to do more than say *Mom*, as if that would stop Laura. The fact they were both obviously uncomfortable with the topic of conversation wasn't stopping her, either.

"I don't know what I'm going to do," she said again. "I came home because I needed my family around me while I have this baby, but I don't know about after. I might not even stay in Stonefield."

She just wanted this conversation to end. Laura shouldn't have brought up her and Lane getting close again while the family was gathered for dinner, and she *definitely* shouldn't have invited her to move in with them. Moving into that house had been the beginning of the end of their marriage, and Laura knew that.

"The apple pies are in," Ellen announced as she walked back into the dining room. "I love the smell of apple pie overlapping the roast turkey smell."

"Did you make chocolate cream pie?" Eli asked, perking up at the mention of pies.

"Of course. And a pumpkin pie, with lots of whipped cream, the way Jack likes it."

Oblivious to the tension in the room, she and Gwen resumed eating, and conversation *not* revolving around Evie's postnatal plans resumed. Her appetite was gone, so she pushed some food around on her plate for a while before putting her fork down. More room for pie, she thought, desperately seeking a silver lining.

Once the meal was over, Evie and her sisters cleared the table. The guys disappeared, of course, and they sent Ellen and Laura to relax for a while. They promised to keep an eye on the pies while they put away leftovers and loaded the dishwasher.

"You're not really going to leave after the baby's born, are you?" Mallory asked after a few minutes of working silently.

"What?" Gwen stopped rummaging through the cupboard for plastic lids. "What are you talking about?"

Evie was silent while Mallory recapped the dinner conversation that had taken place while she was out of the room, and Gwen glared at her. "You can't go."

"I can do what I want," she snapped a second before she realized it was just a knee-jerk reaction to Gwen's bossy tone. "No, I don't want to leave Stonefield again."

"But you said you weren't sure you'd stay in town," Mallory pointed out.

Evie sighed, leaning against the counter. "I know. I was just…trying to keep Laura out of my business, I guess. Asking me to move in with them was too much and with Lane sitting right there? I just wanted the conversation to end."

"Well, it worked," Mallory said. "I don't think Lane's said a word since you said that."

"I'll talk to him. He'll understand." She hoped. He had to see that his mother had stepped over the line, as far as maternal interference went, and maybe Evie had gone too far in pushing back at her, but she didn't plan on going anywhere.

It was almost time for dessert when she realized Case and Irish were watching a football game, but Lane was nowhere in sight. After a quick search showed the bathroom was vacant and he wasn't hovering around the desserts waiting to dig in, she went outside.

She found him in the gazebo, with Boomer curled up on the bench next to him. Case and Gwen had left the dog on the porch, but Lane was his second-favorite human after Case, unless Gwen had taken that spot from him.

"What are you doing out here?" she asked, sitting on the other side of him after giving Boomer a neck scratch. "It's cold."

"Just cooling off. It's hot in the house."

She smiled at the familiar complaint, but he didn't share her amusement. "What's going on with you?"

"What do you mean?" He tried to throw the question out casually, but she could see the tension in his face and his attempt at a smile didn't cause even a single crinkle around his eyes.

"You know what I mean. You haven't spoken to me since dinner."

He shrugged one shoulder. "I didn't want to interrupt if you were planning the fun places you're going to run off to after the baby's born."

"I wasn't running off to fun places, Lane."

"Your Instagram account would say otherwise."

She tried to squash the sense of satisfaction and pleasure she got from knowing he'd obviously been creeping on her feed, but it wasn't easy. "I wasn't running *to* those places as much as I was running *away* from Stonefield—from *us*."

"There hasn't been an *us* since the first time you left."

"I can't believe you just said that with a straight face," she snapped, waving her hand to draw his attention to the baby he seemed to have forgotten they'd made not so long ago. "And what have we been doing this whole time?"

"I don't know," he snapped, shaking his head. "I thought we were working toward something, but then I heard you're not sure if you're going to stick around, so I guess not."

"Lane, you know I just said that so your mother would leave me alone. I mean, what was that? I'm sitting right next to you and Laura invites me to move in with you?" He wasn't the only one who could be angry. "What was I supposed to say? *Your son and I have been having sex for almost two months, but we haven't talked about our future, so thank you for asking me to cohabitate with him?*"

"And threatening to leave Stonefield was the only alternative? You could have said you plan to live with your mom for a while until you figure it out, but thanks for the offer."

The fight went out of Evie, and suddenly she was just really, really tired. "Fine. You're right, Lane."

She stood and started walking away, but he wasn't finished. "Where are you going?"

"I'm going to get some pie. You can either straighten your face and have some, too, or you can sit out here and be mad at me. I don't care."

When she went inside, she might have closed the front door a little harder than she intended to, and everybody turned to look at her. She managed a tight smile, hoping to reassure everybody that all was well, but she didn't think it worked.

"Did you see Lane while you were out there?" Laura asked. "He's not usually late for dessert."

Evie took a breath and counted to five before answering. Snapping at Laura would only make her feel worse, and it wasn't the older woman's fault. And it was a holiday. "He was playing with Boomer. I'm sure he'll be in soon."

Playing was a stretch. It was more like Lane was sulking and Boomer was using his thigh as a pillow, but that wasn't Evie's problem. If Laura really wanted to find him, she could go out there herself.

She had a mouthful of apple pie when he finally came in, but he didn't even look in her direction. For the rest of the evening, he seemed to be across the room or in a conversation with somebody else. She wasn't sure what she'd say to him anyway, but it annoyed her that he was deliberately avoiding a conversation with her.

Of course she cared. She'd been mad, but she shouldn't have told him she didn't care if he sat out there by himself. But she never got the chance to tell him that, and he left while she was in the bathroom. He didn't even say goodbye.

Black Friday, indeed. Lane turned into the Sutton's driveway and parked next to Evie's beloved Jeep, trying to ignore the ache in his chest. This wasn't going to be one of the happiest days of his life, for sure, but he had to protect his relationship with his child. That had meant luring the only lawyer in town out of his turkey coma with a not-inconsiderable amount of money to get what he needed done the day after Thanksgiving.

He hadn't wanted to do it, but he and Evie had never managed to have a conversation about her habit of leaving town without it escalating into an argument or her walking out the door. The chances what he had to say about his wishes as far as custody went would result in a reasonable compromise were practically zero.

He'd sent a text message to Evie once he got what he needed, asking if she'd be around late afternoon. She said she'd be home, so now he just sent her a simple message.

I'm here.

A few minutes later, she walked out of the house and he got out of his truck with the manila envelope in his hand. She gave him a tentative smile when she saw him, and that ache got worse.

"Why didn't you just come in?" she asked, pulling her cardigan tighter over her rounded stomach.

That's why he was here, he reminded himself. It was all about the baby. "I'm not staying long, and I don't really need your family around for this conversation."

She stilled, her brow furrowing in confusion. "What conversation? What's wrong?"

He handed the envelope to her, his stomach knotting. "Nothing's wrong. But yesterday, when you were talking about not knowing what you want to do after the baby's born, I realized that I need to protect my rights as a father, so I talked to my lawyer and—"

"You have a lawyer? It was just an argument, Lane, but now you have a lawyer?"

The way she said it made it sound more like an

accusation than a question, and he bristled. "Of course I have a lawyer. If I learned one thing while getting the brewery off the ground, it's that I'm not fluent in legalese. I managed to muddle through that, but we're talking about child custody here."

"We are?" She held up the envelope, anger flushing her skin a rosy pink. "Are these custody papers?"

"No, they're just…" He struggled to remember how the lawyer had referred to the document. "It's like a tentative parenting plan. Like a starting place."

"The right starting place probably would have been a conversation with the child's mother."

"I don't think you and I have fully developed those communication skills yet. At least this way it's all on the paper, so I'll get to say everything I need to say, so to speak."

He wasn't going to apologize for looking out for his rights as a father, but he also didn't want to escalate this disagreement into a full-blown argument. That's why he wanted to deliver the papers and leave. It was probably going to get there anyway, once she read the documents, but there was a chance she'd have time to process them and calm down before they talked about what he'd worked out with his lawyer.

But he wasn't ready for her to open the clasp and pull out the paperwork right there in front of him.

He hadn't left quickly enough, and now it was too late. "You can read those later, you know."

She shook her head as she scanned the pages and he knew the exact moment she reached the middle of the second page. Her eyes widened and even as she read the paper, the edge was beginning to crumple in her grip.

"I can't leave the state with the child without your permission?"

"That's pretty standard, Evie."

"Wait. I can't move outside of the Stonefield *School District* without your permission? That is *not* standard, Lane." She held the crumpled paper up, as though demanding he look at it. "What the hell is this?"

"I want my child to grow up here, and to form the same childhood bonds we all did. You can't have that bouncing around from place to place."

"This isn't even about the baby," she snapped. "You're trying to make it so I can't leave Stonefield— so I have to live here for at least eighteen years."

"You can leave whenever you want." He held out his hands in a conciliatory gesture. "You just have to give me custody of the baby before you go."

She stared at him, so angry she wasn't even blinking as her chest heaved, and he took a step toward her. He'd known this part of the co-parenting process was going to upset her, but being this outraged wasn't good for the baby.

"Evie, you need to—"

She threw the papers at him, and he stopped moving as they fluttered to the ground between them. "Leave. Now."

He gestured over his shoulder, toward the brewery, wanting the refuge the brewing cellar offered. "I need to—"

"You need to get off this property is what you need to do." She kicked at the papers. "And take your trash with you."

Before Lane could say anything else, she turned and walked up the porch steps. When she reached the top step, she made a sound that sounded like a cross between a hiccup and a sob, and he started after her. He couldn't walk away and leave her crying like that.

But Mallory stepped outside, holding the door open for Evie. She put her hand on her sister's back as she passed, and then gave Lane a look that made it very clear he was *not* welcome in the Sutton house at this very moment. When Mal didn't even make an effort to smooth things over, it was bad.

He wanted to push—to make them understand he wasn't trying to be a jerk. All he wanted to do was make sure he didn't miss out on any of his child's life because Evie had gotten bored and decided to leave town again. But Mallory was already closing the door. If he tried to get inside to explain and her family got involved, there would be no more neutrality. They'd all be mad at him—Case and Irish included, probably—and it might even cause problems between his mom and Ellen.

If he walked away now, it was just another squabble between him and Evie.

That was a lie, he admitted to himself as he climbed into his truck. This wasn't just another squabble. This one had the potential to be ugly, and to drag both their families into it, but he couldn't take it back now, even if he wanted to. As he pulled out onto the road, he reminded himself he didn't want to—that he didn't have a choice. Evie had a history of leaving and taking his heart with her.

But she wasn't taking his child.

Chapter Sixteen

If you're out braving the Black Friday crowds in the city today and come across a bargain that can't be passed up, share in the comments! And don't forget our local deals. Stop by the Perkin' Up Café and buy a $20 gift card, and you'll get a $5 gift card for yourself! And Dearborn's Market will be having flash sales all day. Find them on Facebook to follow the sales.

—Stonefield Gazette *Facebook Page*

"Evie, what's going on?" Mallory put her hand on Evie's arm, trying to get her to look at her.

But Evie was too upset to form coherent words

and senseless ranting wasn't going to make any-body feel better. With her vision blurred with tears, she didn't want to risk navigating the old hardwood stairs, so she walked straight to the downstairs half bath and closed the door a little harder than she'd intended.

"What did he do, Evie?" Mallory called through the door.

"I'm okay," she managed to yell to her sister in a strangled voice before she sank onto the closed toilet lid and buried her face in her hands.

She wasn't okay.

Lane was never going to forgive her for leaving him. He would never trust her. No matter what happened between them, he was never going to let the past go. She'd been a fool to hope they could move forward—to believe they actually had.

After allowing herself to shed the most urgent of the tears and a few moments to get her breath back, she stood and washed her face with bracingly cold water. Lane was right about one thing: being this upset wasn't good for the baby, so she was going to pull herself together and get through this.

She'd dealt with Lane's emotions before. The shock and unbearable grief of losing his father so suddenly. His denial and anger when she'd told him she was leaving him and filing for divorce. The constant arguing whenever they'd crossed paths over the years. And his cold, silent resentment when she'd told him she was leaving again seven months ago.

She'd get through this, too.

When she finally left the bathroom, Evie wasn't surprised to find her mother and both of her sisters at the kitchen table, reading the papers Mallory must have gathered from the driveway. They all looked up when she entered, and Evie knew she wouldn't be burrowing under her covers any time soon. There was an emergency family meeting in progress. After filling her plastic tumbler with water and grabbing a few cookies from the jar, she pulled out a chair and sat.

"I guess the first thing we need to do is find a lawyer," Ellen said. She sounded tired, and guilt ruined Evie's appetite for the cookies.

"Of course he got the only family lawyer in Stonefield," Gwen said. "So we'll have to find somebody in the city."

"Maybe that's better because Evie's lawyer won't know everybody in this town and can be a total shark without worrying about alienating the neighbors," Mallory pointed out.

Evie wasn't sure how she was supposed to pay for a legal shark, and she didn't have enough emotional bandwidth left to listen to them brainstorm how they'd scrimp and sacrifice to help her. And they would, because that's what mothers and sisters did.

After willing back a second round of tears, she

took a sip of water before saying words her heart was rejecting before she even got them all out. "Maybe I should leave now, while I still can. It'll be harder for him to do this if the baby and I are already far away."

"No," all three women said at the same time.

"You can't leave," Ellen said in a small voice.

It was Gwen, of course, who cut right to the chase. She held up her fingers to tick off her points as she spoke. "One, you leaving Stonefield doesn't terminate his rights, so you're still going to have a legal battle. It'll just be longer, nastier and a lot more expensive. Two, are you never going to come home again? If you do, do we have to worry he'll try to take the baby? We're not setting ourselves up for any made-for-TV stuff here. And three, you don't *want* to leave, Evie. You came back because you want to have your baby here and not all alone somewhere else."

"I don't want to leave," she admitted.

"Why did he do this?" Ellen asked. "I assume you didn't know this was coming, so why go to a lawyer without talking to you? And why now?"

"I guess it's because, when Laura was talking about my future, I wasn't willing to swear an oath to never leave this town again. So he's going to try to make the courts do it for me."

"Not moving the baby out of state is one thing," Gwen said. "But not being able to move out of the school district? I don't think that's going to fly."

"What if they make me give the baby to him?" As soon as Evie said the words, the fear took hold in her heart. "I mean, if you look at my life, I move around all the time and hold temporary jobs and always have just enough money to get by. He's lived in his house for his entire life and owns a family business and everybody in this town loves him."

"I don't," Gwen and Mallory said at the same time.

Evie smiled through her tears. "Maybe not right now, but you really do. And why not? He's a great guy. Even I love him."

There was nothing she could do to hold back the tears, then. Tissues appeared, and she tried to stop because now her mom was crying and she couldn't bear it.

"We were doing so good," she said, the words hard to get out through the sobbing. "We were... together again. We were okay."

"This was really stupid on his part," Gwen said, and when Evie looked at her, she could see her oldest sister had shed a few tears, too, as had Mallory.

This was exactly what she'd been afraid of when she'd come home to help open the brewery, and part of why she'd left seven months ago. She'd been so afraid that the friction between her and Lane would tear the family apart and bring her father's dream toppling down.

"But this isn't a legal document," Gwen continued. "This is typed on his lawyer's letterhead, but you weren't served official papers. Right now, everything can still be talked through."

The back door opened and Irish walked in, taking off his cowboy hat and running his hand through his hair, as he always did. "Did I hear Lane's truck? The boys and I—"

He stopped abruptly, looking at the women around the table and taking in the sniffling and pink noses and crumpled tissues. "I… It can wait."

Turning abruptly on the heel of his battered leather boot, he let the screen door bang on his way out the door.

A bubble of laughter escaped Evie, making her feel a little better. "Poor Irish."

They all laughed together, and then Mallory shook her head. "He's come so far, but a roomful of weeping women is probably never going to be in his comfort zone."

There was so much love in the look Mallory gave the door her husband had just gone through that Evie almost cried again. Her eyes welled up, but dabbing at them with a tissue was enough to keep the tears at bay. She didn't believe for a second she was all cried out, because the baby hormones seemed to supply an endless well of tears, but maybe she'd get a chance to rehydrate before the next crying jag.

Now that the fragile house of cards that was her relationship with Lane had come crashing down around her, she had to face the fact she'd been hoping this time would stick. She'd started to think that maybe they'd come to the place in their lives when they were ready to stop looking back and start building a future together. As more than friends. She'd started to believe they could actually be a family.

"There's nothing we can do about this until Monday," Ellen said. "We don't have to open the taproom again until next week, and Irish can handle anything that needs to be done in the cellar. I know we can't put this out of our minds until then, but we can spend this weekend together as a family, remembering that no matter what, we love each other."

"We're here for you," Mallory said, taking her hand.

Gwen nodded. "No matter what happens, you're not alone."

Evie knew she had their support, but as she looked around at the women who loved her, the guilt threatened to devour her. Her mother's best friend was Lane's mom. Gwen's fiancé was Lane's cousin and best friend. Mallory's husband was Lane's friend and brewing partner.

No matter what, she was the odd one out. And, as she had so many times in her life, she'd really made a mess of everything.

"Lane?" He heard his mother's voice and the tapping on the doorjamb of his open bedroom door and forced himself to look up.

Ouch. When he'd gotten home from the disastrous meeting with Evie, he'd gone straight to his room and dropped into the armchair. Then he'd rested his elbows on his knees, lowered his head into his hands and just…stayed there. Obviously for too long, since his back and neck were not thrilled about straightening.

"What's wrong?" She didn't wait for an invitation, but walked in and crouched in front of him. "Is the baby okay?"

He nodded, and then rubbed his hand across the back of his neck, hoping to ease the ache there. "The baby's fine."

After blowing out a relieved breath, she stood. "Come downstairs and eat."

"I'm not hungry."

"Then I *know* something's wrong. What happened?"

"I had a lawyer make up a parenting plan with a bunch of rules about the baby and gave them to Evie."

"Oh, Lane." The disappointment in her sigh as she sat on the edge of his bed made him wince. "Had you two been talking about it? Was there something you weren't agreeing on?"

"We hadn't talked about it at all. I panicked," he admitted. "When she said she wasn't sure what she was doing after the baby's born, I thought about what it would feel like if she took off again and took the baby with her and I just wanted to stop that from happening."

"So you blindsided her with legal documents?"

"I mean, they're not official or anything. It's just what I want, written on the lawyer's letterhead." When she arched an eyebrow at him, he sighed. "I handled it badly."

"I assume she didn't take it well."

"She threw the papers on the ground and told me to leave and take my trash with me."

To his surprise, the corner of her mouth lifted. "That sounds like Evie. Being thrown off the property will make things difficult for you, though."

"I don't care." He shoved his hand through his hair and blew out a breath. "Evie and I were doing so well and now I'll be lucky if she ever speaks to me again. This isn't what I wanted."

"Then you need to fix it. You need to apologize— tell her you overreacted and you need to tell her *why*. You've never gotten over her leaving you and you keep punishing her for it."

"I'm not… I don't mean to. But she's going to have my baby and she has a habit of leaving. Me acting like an ass doesn't make that not true."

"I didn't want to marry your father." She sucked in a quick breath, as if saying the words actually hurt her, and he was confused by the sudden shift in the conversation. "I loved him, I guess, as much as a girl that age can be in love. But before I was even legally an adult, I had a husband and a baby.

It wasn't long after you were born that your dad and uncle started the tree service, and then I was an unpaid receptionist and bookkeeper on top of everything else."

Hearing what his unplanned arrival had done to her life made Lane feel a little sad, but he also knew she had no regrets where he was concerned. There had never been a day in his life he'd felt anything but unconditionally loved by her. He didn't like knowing she'd been unhappy, though.

"That was my life for over twenty years, and they were good years. Joe and I were happy enough, and he provided well for us. But after he died and the grieving faded some, I realized I answer to nobody now, and I like it that way."

"If you want to go do something else, Mom, say the word. We can hire somebody to run the office."

She laughed, waving a hand. "No, you won't. I enjoy being a part of the company still, and of what you and Case are doing. And also, unlike your father and your uncle, you two pay me for my work."

"Then why are you telling me this?"

"Because I'm your mother and I am one-hundred-percent Team Lane in all things, but there's a little piece of my heart that feels for what Evie went through." When he opened his mouth, she made a gesture with her hand to tell him to zip it. "The reason you two moved into that cheap, hideous rental when you got married was because you were going to travel for a while before you settled down, and you didn't know if it would even be in Stonefield. You two had big dreams. Four months later your father died and everything changed."

"And she left me," he reminded her.

"Not right away, though. You stepped up, working with your uncle and Case. And Evie helped me out in the office, because I was having a hard time. Such a hard time, actually, that you decided you would both move back into the house."

"Did you think I would just walk away?" His voice shook slightly, but he was careful to keep his voice low because this was his mother he was talking to.

"No, but you changed your entire life and I don't think you gave Evie much of a voice. And that just became the way it was. You settled into a new life, running your father's half of the business and expecting her to work in the office and accept this was your home now. It wasn't the life she signed up for."

"I didn't sign up for Dad dying."

"None of us did, but *months* went by, Lane. I learned to be okay. But you'd made a new life, and you shut Evie out. You wouldn't even have a conversation about the future you'd planned with *her*. You didn't try to compromise. By the time eight months rolled around, I think she realized that the life she was living then was going to be the *rest* of her life and she wasn't happy with that. So she left."

Lane didn't know what to say to that because he couldn't remember having any other choice. He remembered the shock of his mother calling to tell him his father was dead. Then trying to keep his and his mother's heads above water as wave after wave of grief tried to pull them under. Evie had been so supportive at first, but then she'd started pulling away. Eventually, she lost interest and took off.

"And one more thing," his mom said.

"I don't want to talk about this anymore."

"I have one more thing to say and you're going to listen because I'm your mother." She gave him a look that practically dared him to get up and walk away, but he didn't. "Yes, Evie left you. But you need to *really* think about that year and ask yourself if she left because the man she fell in love with and married had already left *her*."

He wasn't sure what to say to that.

Lane didn't *want* to really think about that year. It wasn't merely the darkest year of his life. It was practically a black hole and the last thing he wanted to do was wallow in it again. Losing his father and his marriage had left an emotional wound he preferred not to poke at. It hurt, and replaying the entire year sounded like hell.

But his mother wouldn't have said those words lightly, so if he really wanted to have peace with Evie, maybe he needed to take a more critical look at his own role in their divorce. "I'll think about what you've said."

"Good. Now I'm going to make us something to eat." She stood and walked to the door, where she paused. "I'm a little surprised Ellen hasn't called me yet."

He really hoped his mother's friendship with Evie's mom wouldn't be collateral damage. "They're probably trying to figure out if Irish can handle the brewery alone."

"That's not going to happen. You might have to park on the other side of the building, in the customer lot, for a little while, but you guys will get through this. The taproom's closed for a few days, so let Irish handle things in the cellar and give everybody some time to calm down. It's going to be okay. Let's go eat now."

He got up and dutifully followed her to the kitchen, but he had his doubts that everything was going to be okay. Things would get sorted with the brewery, one way or another. He was sure his relationship with Ellen and Irish would survive this blow, at the very least, even if he had to limit his involvement to the brewing and let Irish man the bar alone for a while. There was even a possibility that he and Evie would work through the damage and eventually come to an amicable co-parenting agreement.

But the relationship he'd been building with Evie—the fragile hope that they might actually have a future together—was shattered and this time he was the one who'd broken it.

She was never going to forgive him for this.

Chapter Seventeen

The High Street saga has come to an end (and we mean it this time). Effective immediately, High Street is renamed Hill Street. A committee comprised of our selectman, our fire and police chiefs (who were seen having coffee together this morning) and the road's residents agreed the name is boring enough to deter our town's intrepid stolen street sign collectors, and technically there is a slight incline before the Gordons' property. The vote was unanimous and the sign has been ordered. According to Chief Bordeaux, "Any residents who don't like it can...[redacted]...just leave me alone."

      —Stonefield Gazette *Facebook Page*

"Evie, you can't keep doing the fun parts. You have to do some of the sky, too." It was the third time Gwen had said it, and it was going to be the third time Evie ignored her. She hated jigsaw puzzles with a lot of sky, even if they were Christmas themed.

"Give her a break," Mallory said. "She's had a rough couple of days."

"I know she has, but it's still not fair that she's getting to do the best parts of the Christmas village while two hundred identical blue pieces have to be put together."

"You know I can hear you, right?" Evie picked up a blue piece just to mollify Gwen.

"It's Monday," Ellen said. "Have you made a decision about what you want to do?"

"No." And it wasn't for lack of trying. Even though she'd spent the weekend with her family, doing puzzles and baking and cleaning up the yard with the boys, some part of her mind was always preoccupied with the problem of what to do about Lane. "I know I should start calling lawyers, but I just hate the idea of having to communicate with him through our attorneys about everything."

Mallory slid a small section of sky into place with a grunt of satisfaction. "Maybe you don't need a lawyer quite yet."

"I don't want to be in the middle of this," Gwen said, "but I've gotten the impression from Case that maybe Lane regrets having brought a lawyer into it without talking to you first. And that's all I know and all I'm saying."

Evie wanted to press her sister for more details, but she stopped herself. Gwen was in a tough spot, and Evie had made things hard enough on her without trying to make her share anything else Case may have told her in confidence.

"See?" Ellen gave her a reassuring smile. "You just need to talk to him and sort things out."

"I can't talk to him," Evie said, frustration making her voice loud in the room.

"Then write him a letter," Gwen suggested.

Evie rolled her eyes. "Oh sure, I'll just slip a note in his locker before lunch."

"I'm serious, Evie. Write it down. Even if you don't give it to him—although you definitely should—it'll help."

After they took a break for lunch, Evie opted out of the trip to buy wreaths for the brewery and the house. The boys were excited about the trip, hoping they could talk Mallory into getting the Christmas tree early, but Evie didn't have the energy to keep up with all of them today.

She tried to nap, but she couldn't put Lane out of her mind. Finally, with Gwen's advice running around her head, she found a sheet of paper and a pen and sat down to pour her heart onto the page. It took her almost an hour to write the short letter because she had to keep stopping to wipe the tears off her cheeks so they wouldn't fall on the paper and make the ink run.

Lane,
Gwen suggested I write you a letter because I didn't know how to talk to you, so I'm going to try it.

Sometimes I wonder how two people who loved each other so much can barely have a civil conversation now, and why seeing you brings out the worst in me. I guess it's because it makes me remember the worst decision I ever made. When I see you, I remember the love first. I always will.

Then I remember the pain. I broke both of our hearts when I left, but I was young and I wasn't ready for the life you had decided we were going to live. So when I see you, it hurts. I feel shame and regret and sadness, and I don't like feeling bad. It makes me lash out at you, and I'm sorry for that.

I should have tried harder to tell you how unhappy I was in our marriage. You should have listened. And you should have talked to me about custody before talking to a lawyer. I can forgive you for that because I know why you though you couldn't. We can't keep try-ing to move forward while the past is still a wedge between us.

We need to find a way to forgive each

*other. I need to forgive you and forgive my-
self. And I need you to forgive me for leaving.
Evie*

Before she could talk herself out of it, she folded
the letter and sealed it in an envelope. Then she
scrawled his name on the front and grabbed her
keys. His truck was parked in his yard, but the lot
where they parked the tree service trucks and equipment was empty, so she knew he was still out on a
job. She preferred it that way, since she didn't want
to see him. She just wanted to leave the envelope
in the mailbox and drive away.

She didn't sleep well that night, tossing and turning as she thought about the words she'd written to
Lane. It was the most honest she'd ever been in her
life, and all she could do was wait and see how he'd
respond. Or if he would at all.

It was the possibility that he might ignore the letter entirely that had kept her awake, and once everybody had left for the day—the boys to school,
her mom and Mallory to the thrift shop and Irish to
the cellar—she'd crawled back into bed.

Sleep didn't come, however, so she was awake
when her phone chimed. Expecting it to be one of
her sisters checking on her, she snaked her arm out
of the warm bedding nest and snagged the device
off the nightstand. Her pulse quickened when the
notification on the lock screen told her the text message was from Lane.

Can I stop by so we can talk?

Tears were already gathering in her eyes, even though she had no idea if they'd be having a good talk or a not-so-good talk. At least he'd reached out. You're not working?

I didn't sleep last night, so chainsaws seemed like a bad idea.

So he'd tossed and turned, too. It shouldn't make her feel better, but it did. I'm home, so you can stop by any time.

I'm on my way.

That didn't leave her a lot of time to clean up and get dressed, so she'd just gotten downstairs when she heard his truck pull into the driveway. Every muscle in her body felt knotted up and she forced herself to stop and take a few deep breaths before she slid her coat on and shoved her feet into Mallory's boots, just because they were next to the door.

Nobody else was home, but she still wasn't inviting Lane into the house until she had some idea of what he wanted to talk about. He was almost to the steps when she walked out onto the porch and pulled the door closed behind her.

"Can we go sit in the gazebo?" he asked, shoving his hands in the pockets of his zip-up D&T Tree

Service sweatshirt. "I know it's on the chilly side, but it's still a nice day."

It was also a quick walk to his truck if things went sideways on them, but she didn't point that out. There was no sense in putting that kind of energy out there if she could help it. "Yeah."

They didn't talk during the short walk to the gazebo, and as she sat on the bench, she watched him pull a folded-up sheet of paper from the back pocket of his jeans. For a moment, she thought he'd come to bring her letter back to her, but then she noticed it was a different kind of paper.

"I was going to read this to you, but..." The words were strangled by the emotion choking them off and he cleared his throat. "I can't."

He held out the paper, sitting next to her on the bench. Not close enough to touch, but close enough so she could take the paper from him. She unfolded it and sucked in a breath when she saw his large, messy handwriting filling the page.

Evie,
When my father died, I felt like my choices were taken away. I had to stay and take his place in the business because that was his legacy and it also provided for my mother. I was determined to put away my grief and make a good life for us, but I took your choice away, too. It wasn't the life you wanted, so you left.

I've blamed you for leaving me for the last

ten years, but my mom said something that's made me really think about what happened and here's the truth: I was afraid to have a conversation with you about our future because I was afraid I'd have to choose between you and my mom, so I refused to talk about it at all. I see now that I didn't know what to do, so I put you in the position of having to be the bad guy. I made you the villain of our fairy tale but the truth is that fairy tales aren't real. We're all just people trying to do our best and I let you down. I let us down. And I was afraid of letting the baby down, so I panicked and talked to a lawyer instead of talking to you. I'm sorry.

   I forgive you for leaving, but I need you to forgive me for putting you in the position where you had no other choice.
Lane

It was going to be a while before she could get any words past the lump of emotion in her throat, so she scooted down the bench and held out her hand. He scooted the rest of the distance between them before lacing his fingers through hers and resting their joined hands on his thigh.

They sat in silence for a few minutes, his thumb stroking hers, while Evie tried to absorb everything he'd written to her. She'd been honest with him and he'd responded in kind, and maybe truth could finally lay the pain of the past to rest.

"I'm sorry," he said in a rough voice. "It's in the letter, but I want to say it out loud to you. I'm sorry I drove you out of our marriage."

"I'm sorry I left." She used her free hand to swipe at her eyes before turning to face him. "We were young, Lane. I forgive you for shutting me out."

His face crumpled a little and he had to clear his throat before he could get the words out. "I forgive you for leaving."

She wiped a tear from his cheek with her thumb, and he smiled so sweetly, her breath caught in her throat. Then she stood and tugged on his hand until he did the same so she could wrap him in a hug. His arms went around her and he squeezed, his face pressed to her hair.

It felt so good she couldn't help crying again, and he held her until it finally stopped, occasionally pressing kisses to her hair.

"You can wipe your face on my sweatshirt if you want," he said when the tears had passed. "I'll pretend I didn't notice."

She chuckled, pulling tissues out of her pocket to mop at her face. "I have tissues in every pocket these days."

"I'm sorry I made you cry." He stepped back and pushed a strand of hair back from her damp cheek. "And I'm more sorry than I can say about the papers. I handled that really badly. I thought about you leaving and taking the baby and I panicked."

"I have no plans to leave Stonefield, Lane. When Laura started talking about the future, I was afraid to say anything about us because I wasn't sure what we were doing, and…well, I panicked."

He chuckled, his eyes warm as he looked into hers. "Let's stop panicking and feeling guilty and be friends again."

"I'd like that."

"Good." He inhaled deeply, and then shoved his hands in his pockets again. "I'm going to go now, because this was a lot and we can probably both use a little time to process."

"And to nap. I haven't slept well, either."

"Definitely a nap." He cleared his throat, and she could tell by the hint of color in his cheeks that he was thinking about them napping together.

But things were too raw between them right now. They'd shone a light on some old hurts and the healing could start, but ending up in bed together right now would be a mistake. It was a shame, too, since nobody else was home.

"I'm never going to hear the end of this from Gwen," she said, and then she grinned. "She does love to be right."

"She was right about the letters," he admitted. "And my mom, too. She dropped some wisdom on my head when she found out what I did. I'm thankful it wasn't a frying pan, though. She probably thought about it."

"It was worth it because now we're in a new place," Evie said, thankful she didn't start bawling again. "Now we can go forward without looking back."

His mouth quirked into a smile and the difference in his expression was like a jolt of electricity making her pulse quicken. The Lane she'd fallen in love with so long ago was back, with no reservation lurking under the surface. No unspoken accusations and no wariness. And she didn't feel the pangs of shame and guilt. There was just the only man she'd ever loved, and the sparkle in his eyes.

"I'm looking forward to it," he said. "Oh, and maybe you could tell Ellen and your sisters it's okay if I'm here when the taproom reopens day after tomorrow so they don't have Irish and Case run me off."

She laughed. "I'll tell them."

"Okay, so… I guess I'll see you later, then."

She stopped herself from grabbing the front of his sweatshirt and hauling him in for a long, hungry kiss. He was right—they both had a lot to process. But it wasn't easy to let him go. "Yeah. See you later."

When he got to the edge of the gazebo steps, he turned back. "Would you maybe go to dinner with me tomorrow night?"

She smiled. "Like a date, you mean?"

"I definitely mean like a date."

A thrill of anticipation made her feel like a kid again. "I'd love to."

The next evening, Lane leaned forward, wishing Evie was sitting next to him instead of across from him in the booth. "Why am I so nervous?"

"Because it's our first date," she replied with a chuckle.

"It does feel like that." From the moment he'd opened his eyes that morning, he'd had trouble thinking about anything but having dinner with Evie. He'd been so distracted, Case had taken his chain saw away and assigned him to dragging brush to the chipper with the young kid who worked for them.

It didn't matter that he'd loved this woman since they were kids, or that they'd already done this part—the first date right through walking down the aisle. They'd gone through a divorce. They were having a baby together. But there was something about *this* date and how it was a new beginning for them that made it feel special.

"We should have driven to the city," he said, realizing too late that he might not have made this special enough for her. "I could have gotten reservations or something."

Laughing, she reached across the table to cover his hand with hers. "Stop. This is fine, and I'm glad we're here because it won't be much longer before I don't fit into the booth."

"You get more beautiful every day." He meant it, and he hoped she knew that.

When his phone chimed, she laughed. "And we weren't even kissing this time."

After reading the text message, he grinned at Evie. "It's from my mom. She's going over to your house to go through some knitting patterns with Ellen and she'll probably be hours."

The way Evie looked at him seemed to raise the temperature in the diner by twenty degrees. "We could get this to go."

"Again?" He chuckled. "They're going to start serving us in to-go containers, just in case."

"Do you care?"

"No." He didn't even care if they left without the food. They had stuff to eat at home. While the idea of going on a real date had been nice, the thought of having her in his bed was a lot nicer. But then he sighed because his heart was actually going to override other parts of his body. That didn't happen often.

But this night had felt special to him and, while any time he got to make love to Evie was also special, he wanted to continue feeling the way he'd felt before he'd gotten the text message from his mother. Falling into bed came easily to them. He wanted to savor the newness of being together fully clothed and without the past lurking just under the surface.

"There's plenty of time," he said. "Let's enjoy our date and then we can go to my place and... enjoy it some more."

Her smile lit up her eyes, and he knew he'd made the right call. It was so right, actually, that they lingered—talking and laughing and taking their time with their meals. It was almost like when they were young, except it was better.

Now they were older and, thanks to Gwen's suggestion they write the words they were struggling to say, they were wiser. They'd gone through the wringer—put each other through it—and they'd come together as adults who were choosing each other. While he'd always loved her, losing her and the years spent alone had given him a deeper appreciation for what that meant, and for her.

By the time they reached his house, he knew it wouldn't be long until his mother arrived home. "Is that a problem? I mean... I..."

She laughed. "It's not a problem for me. We're adults and it's a big house. And it wouldn't be the first time, you know."

It wasn't the first time, but it was the best time. With the shadows of the past chased away, he was free to bask in her sunshine-like warmth. They made love in his bed, and he ran his hands over her body. He was gentle with her breasts because they were sensitive and despite reading a stack of library books, he wasn't totally sure if it was a good sensitive or a sore sensitive. Instead he concentrated on stroking every other inch of her. He rubbed her back, and they laughed when she arched against him and the baby kicked.

It was a new experience for both of them, and a little distracting, but one important fact he *had* gleaned from the books was that sex wouldn't hurt the baby and that orgasms were good for her. They'd be good for him, too, but he used his tongue to make sure she had one before he went looking for his own.

When he sprawled on his back and she straddled him, it took all of Lane's self-control to keep his hands loose on her hips and let her guide his erection into her. She took him in slowly, finding her own comfort level, and he breathed a sigh of relief and anticipation when he was finally buried inside her. She rocked her hips, setting the pace, and he never would have guessed that the feeling of having to restrain himself could feel so good. But it did. Good enough so he stroked her clit with his thumb until she rocked hard and faster and came with a moan of pleasure that was his undoing.

The orgasm hit him hard and his hips jerked, but he gripped her thighs and held her up so he wasn't driving into her. Then his body went liquid and he wrapped his arms around her as she collapsed on top of him, sliding slightly to the side to accommodate her stomach.

He couldn't stop kissing and stroking her hair, even as his eyelids got heavy. He wasn't sure if he nodded off, but at some point she slid out of bed. He was going to protest and, if she tried to get dressed, beg her to stay. But then she returned, sliding under the covers and pressing her warm back against his chest.

She stayed the night, and nothing in Lane's life had ever felt as good as waking up next to her, his arm curved around her stomach. They cuddled for a while, content to stay under the covers, until Evie smelled bacon. His mom had made breakfast, and it felt wonderful not to tiptoe around their family anymore.

Not that there were any more hints about Evie moving in—not yet anyway. His mom seemed to sense that this happy place he and Evie were in was new and fragile, and they just wanted to enjoy being emotionally free to love each other again.

For right now, it was enough.

Chapter Eighteen

As you might recall, we're collecting the things you love most about Stonefield or small towns in general to prepare for luring a new librarian to our town next year. To the anonymous person who submitted "the best thing about living in a small town is how many people still use clotheslines, so we all know what kind of underwear our neighbors wear," Chief Bordeaux would like to remind you that you can look, but you can't touch! We hope you understand we won't be using your submission in our presentations to the candidates.

—Stonefield Gazette *Facebook Page*

"**I** don't understand why I can't go in what I'm wearing." Evie looked at her reflection in the mirror, seeing nothing wrong with a very oversize flannel shirt hanging open over a T-shirt and leggings. Getting custom Sutton's Place maternity T-shirts wouldn't be cheap, so she'd given up on that idea and wore whatever she was comfortable in. The customers didn't care.

Mallory dropped her head and sighed. "I *told* you, a writer for a major magazine might be stopping by to check us out and we want to make a good impression."

"Hopefully the article will be about the beer and not my flannel shirt."

"Evie, please? This is important to Mom."

Evie frowned. It would also be important to Lane and to Irish. With a weary sigh, she surrendered. "Fine, I'll change. But only because you caught me while I'm still upstairs. If I'd already gone down, I would have let the brewery go down in flames from the shame of my flannel shirt before I climbed those stairs again."

"I'll meet you out there. I want to do a final check and make sure everything's perfect. Oh, and maybe a little lip gloss. Some mascara even? Just in case he wants to take photos of you serving customers."

Evie rolled her eyes and went back to her closet. There wasn't much to choose from, but eventually she chose a soft navy sweater to go over the leggings. Those, she wasn't changing. The sweater hugged her very pregnant figure more than she would have liked, but the color was a close match to the Sutton's Place T-shirts. She even took her hair out of its messy bun and brushed it into a sleek ponytail before putting on the bare minimum of makeup.

That was as good as it was going to get, she thought as she made her way slowly down the stairs. It wasn't a long walk across the driveway to work, so she didn't bother with a coat. Instead she shoved her feet into the slip-on booties that were supportive while still being somewhat cute. Or at least not ugly.

There were more cars in the lot than she expected so early. They often had people waiting for them to open the doors, but not this many. Maybe it was the stress of Christmas being not too far away. Or maybe word had leaked that a magazine writer was going to make an appearance and they were all hoping for a shot at fame, Stonefield style. She wondered how many people who'd grumbled about imagined similarities to the characters in Gwen's books would line up to be mentioned in an article about Sutton's Place Brewery & Tavern.

But when she opened the door and stepped inside, a chorus of "Surprise!" went up and she put her hand to her chest, thankful she'd gone pee recently.

There were pastel balloons everywhere, along with streamers, and it took her a few seconds to realize this was her baby shower. And everybody she loved was in the taproom, even her nephews, who were jumping up and down a little too close to the tiered cake with the porcelain pacifier on top.

Her mother hugged her first, and then she was surrounded by her family and friends. Even some of the regular customers were there, though it was obvious they'd somehow spread the word they were having a private event without her finding out.

When Mallory hugged her, she spoke softly near Evie's ear. "I think you look gorgeous in flannel with your messy hair, but Mom and Laura are going to take at least three hundred pictures of you tonight."

"Each." She squeezed her sister. "Thank you."

Then Lane was there, and she got a little teary-eyed when he took her hand in his. "Did we really manage to keep this a secret from you? You didn't know?"

"No, I had no idea. I swear."

Case laughed. "I think that's the first secret the Sutton women have ever kept."

As the crowd laughed, Lane led her toward the side wall of the taproom where the tables had been cleared away. Evie knew from experience they wouldn't be having her sit in front of the glass wall because it was a horrible backdrop for taking pictures.

But she didn't expect to see the glider rocker—the one she'd fallen in love with at Sutton's Seconds.

There were ribbons tied on to it, as well as a large tag. She had to blink away tears before she could read the words scrawled on it.

For rocking our baby. Love, Lane.

A few of those tears got away from her, sliding over her cheeks as she threw her arms around his neck. He kissed her cheek before holding her tight. "Your sisters helped me shop."

"It's perfect, Lane."

With a reluctant sigh only she could hear, he pulled back and swept his arm toward the rocker. "Your throne, milady."

She thought he was just being funny, but then Molly appeared with a sparkly tiara, which she put on Evie's head. Thank goodness she'd brushed her hair properly, she thought. Not that anybody in this room would love her any less if her tiara got tangled in a mass of messy bun, but photos were forever and she and Mallory had been right. She wasn't sure her mother or Laura had stopped hitting their shutter buttons since she walked in.

Jack and Eli stepped forward and made awkward attempts at courtly bows, and it was Eli who spoke. "Aunt Evie, we're your... What was the word?"

"Court jesters," Irish said, and everybody laughed.

"That wasn't it," Jack said.

"Are you my courtiers?" Evie asked.

"That's it," Jack said. "We're going to help you with your presents."

There were a *lot* of presents, and she needed all

the help she could get. Jack and Eli would bring them to her. Gwen had a notebook, of course, and she carefully jotted down names and gifts, and she would probably start nagging Evie about thank-you cards before lunch tomorrow. And Mallory was sticking bows to a paper plate, which seemed odd, but she didn't know a lot about baby showers.

"This one doesn't have a card," Eli said, holding a small box out to her.

"That one's from me," Lane said, and Evie looked up at him.

"Lane, the glider was so much."

"Just open it."

Evie had heard the slight gasps from the women in the crowd—namely Ellen and Laura—and she'd felt a moment of anxiety, but the box was too big to hold the gift their mothers were probably hoping for. And she didn't want to get that gift at her baby shower, in front of everybody.

After carefully peeling back the paper, she saw it was a very ornate cardboard box. And when she opened the lid, she saw the most decadent chocolates she'd ever seen.

Lane leaned down close. "Bonbons for my lady."

Evie laughed and closed the box so she could hug it to her chest. "Where did you find these?"

"I might suck at social media, but I know how to use the internet."

"I don't want to share with everybody, so I'm going to save them for later." She smiled when he gave her a cheeky grin. "I might share with you, though."

Once the presents were open and she'd shed a few more tears at how generous her friends and family were, they cut the cake and everybody mingled for a while. Then there were games, which Molly was in charge of, naturally.

They laughed their way through one particularly interesting game in which contestants had to guess what was smeared on a diaper based on only sight and smell. Nobody was surprised when Irish was the first to guess the one with barbecue sauce, and the one with melted chocolate was an easy one. The diapers with the mashed peas and the mustard were a little harder—and more gruesome— and Evie didn't like how many mothers in the room nodded and said, *"Yup, I remember those days."*

The evening was dwindling to a close—in no small part because the mother-to-be was utterly exhausted and crashing after her third slice of cake— when Ellen picked up the paper plate covered in bows.

"You have to toss this," she said, holding it out to Evie.

"Toss it? What was the point of collecting the bows just to throw it away?"

"No, toss it like a bouquet. When the bride tosses her bouquet at her wedding, whoever catches it is the next bride. When the expectant mother tosses *her* bouquet at her baby shower, whoever catches it will be the next one pregnant."

Most of the women in the room scattered to the shadows of the far corners of the taproom, and Evie laughed as she took the paper plate and looked at the handful of women left in the center of the taproom.

"Wait, where's Mallory?"

"I already have two, Evie. Those jesters who are wired on sugar, remember?"

"Courtiers," Eli yelled.

"But—" And then Evie snapped her mouth closed because she didn't know who else in the room Mallory had told about trying to get pregnant. She didn't want to make it awkward for her and Irish.

Then Irish looked down at Mallory, who had her arm looped through her husband's and was smiling up at him. When she gave a little nod, he lifted his hat to swipe his hand over his hair in a now-familiar nervous gesture, and then he grinned. "And we've already got a third jester on the way, so it only seems fair to give somebody else a chance."

The paper plate was temporarily forgotten while everybody congratulated the happy couple. Ellen cried again, and Evie really hoped her mother was drinking a lot of water because the poor woman was going to end up dehydrated.

"Our kids will be so close in age," Evie said when it was finally her turn to hug her sister.

"They're going to be cousins and friends, just like Lane and Case."

And then Gwen caught the paper plate bouquet and Ellen cried again.

"Is there like a dating bouquet?" Molly asked. "Like maybe a woman goes on a wonderful date and then she tosses her popcorn bucket or table centerpiece and whoever catches it finds a really great guy to date."

"You're not helping clean up," Gwen told Evie once the nonfamily guests had left. "Take your bonbons and your man and go in the house."

Lane didn't go inside with her, though. He stopped her on the porch and cupped her face in his hands. "You're so exhausted, you're practically weaving. Go inside and get some sleep."

She wanted to argue with him. The night had been so perfect and so much fun, but he wasn't wrong. She couldn't remember the last time she'd been this tired. "I'm not going to eat my first bonbon until we're together."

"Tomorrow," he promised.

"Thank you for my rocking chair, Lane." She felt tears gathering again and tried to blink them away. She was almost as bad as her mother. "I really do love it."

"I'm glad." He leaned in and kissed her softly before stroking his hand over the curve of her stomach. "Good night, milady."

"Good night, sweet prince." He gave her a fake

look of outrage and she laughed. "Fine. Good night, my king."

He kissed her again and then offered her a low bow before nodding toward the house.

"I would curtsy, but…that would probably be a disaster."

She could still hear his chuckle as he walked to his truck and she closed the door behind her. For a moment she leaned back against the wood, smiling to herself. She was exhausted, really had to pee and had some regrets about the amount of sugar she'd consumed tonight, but none of that mattered because she was also the happiest she'd ever been.

"This was probably not the sexiest date you've ever been on."

Lane squeezed her hand, feeling the warmth through the soft gloves she wore. "You're wrong about that. Getting to play hooky on a Tuesday to visit the baby doctor with you is incredibly sexy. Everything about you is."

Her laughter turned heads and he just shrugged because he meant every word of it. With every date they'd gone on over the last ten days, he felt more and more in love with her. They'd been simple dates, of course. She was very pregnant, there wasn't a lot to do in Stonefield and it was already cold outside. But they'd had a movie night and taken a drive into the city to do some Christmas shopping. They'd even had a candlelight dinner on Monday night, when the taproom was closed, just to enjoy the quiet—and private—ambience of the place.

This date was a trip to the doctor's office for a checkup, and hearing their baby's heartbeat made him happier than he would have thought possible. They went to lunch after the appointment, and then she wanted to stop by the thrift shop because Ellen had gotten in a stroller she thought Evie might like.

They had to park quite a distance from the store, but Evie insisted walking was good for her and it was a nice day. He kept a slow pace, not only because she had shorter legs, but because he enjoyed walking hand in hand with her. People they passed greeted them, and more than a few noticed their joined hands and smiled, which he liked. It was nice to know people were rooting for them.

They were a little more than halfway when she suddenly stopped walking. She didn't put her hand to her stomach or anything, so he didn't think it was the baby, but he was concerned by how still she was.

"Evie, what's wrong? Is it the baby?"

"This is the life I want."

He wasn't sure he'd heard her correctly. "What are you saying?"

She turned to face him, looking up with tears shimmering in her eyes. "I mean that, Lane. This—you and I together, making a life *together*—is all I've ever wanted."

"*You* are all I've ever wanted."

"Why are we dating? I love you, Lane. I always

have. I always will." She laughed. "It feels silly going on dates like this. Dating is for finding the one, but you're the one, and you always have been."

"I love you, Evie. I've never stopped loving you."

They were blocking part of the sidewalk, but he didn't care. They could go around. Or they could stand there and watch. All he cared about was the love of his life looking at him with her heart in her eyes.

"Marry me again, Evie." The words surprised them both, but he meant them with his whole heart and he wouldn't take them back.

"Yes," she said, without hesitation. "Yes, I want to marry you and spend the rest of my life with you."

His heart was hammering in his chest as he looked into the depths of her blue eyes. All he saw there was the same love and joy he was feeling. "I don't have your ring yet. I'm supposed to pick it up two days before Christmas, which was cutting it close."

She laughed. "I wouldn't be able to get it on my finger right now anyway."

"Maybe we can find a little place to rent, or even buy a house of our own." His mind was whirling with the promise of their future together.

She smiled, pressing her hand to his cheek. "And leave Laura bouncing around that big house by herself? Plus, all of the tree service's equipment is there. It doesn't make any sense to buy another house."

"We'll take the whole upstairs, then. We'll have our bedroom and a room for the baby, and we can turn the other bedroom into a living room or whatever so you have a space of your own."

"Whatever we do, we'll figure it out together. And we're not going to figure it all out today. All that matters right now is that you and I are going to spend the rest of our lives together, madly in love."

"Damn right we are." He was still grinning, and he couldn't make himself stop. "Will you stay with me while we figure it out? I don't want to spend another night without you. *Ever.*"

"Yes. I want to wake up in your bed every morning." She glanced down the street and then laughed, turning back to him. "Don't look now, but we have an audience."

He looked and sure enough, standing on the sidewalk in front of Sutton's Seconds, phone pressed to her ear, was Ellen Sutton. "What do you think the chances are she's talking to *my* mom?"

"Oh, one hundred percent. She looks very emotional, so either something really big is happening behind us, or somebody went in and told her we're out here getting engaged on Main Street."

Lane made a show of looking over his shoulder, which made her laugh. "Must be us. Should we give her something to tell *my* mom?"

"What do you have in mind?"

He grinned, and then raised his arms as he yelled, "She said yes! Again!"

And then, as their fellow pedestrians applauded—but not loudly enough to drown out Ellen's excited squeal—Lane cradled the baby bump with one hand and the back of Evie's neck with the other, and kissed his ex and future wife.

Epilogue

January 25th

Evie walked into the dining room, where most of the family was gathered around the table, working on a jigsaw puzzle. Of course, now that she was too pregnant with a stubborn child who refused to get out of her to maintain jigsaw puzzle posture for more than two minutes, they'd bought one with no sky.

"It's time," she said, and all the heads swiveled in her direction.

"The timer didn't go off. The lasagna still has at least twenty minutes," her mom said.

"No, it's *time*. For the baby."

"We're in the middle of a winter storm," Gwen said, as if the mix of snow and freezing rain wasn't the reason they were all doing the puzzle.

"Well, my water broke, so I don't think I'm getting a snow day."

"Oh no," Ellen said, which wasn't really the level of excitement she'd expected from her mother when the time finally came. "Laura and I were afraid of this. The barometric pressure or something can trigger labor."

"I'm glad something finally did," Evie muttered. Sure the weather outside was frightful, but this baby was a week overdue and Evie had passed from uncomfortable to miserable several weeks ago.

"Okay," Lane said, pushing back his chair and standing. "We knew this was a possibility. It's January in New England. So we made a plan."

"Yes, we did," Gwen said. Evie figured her sister had probably written it out in one of her many notebooks.

"Does anybody remember the plan?" Lane asked, and Evie realized Lane looked calm and collected, but he was freaking out internally.

"I'm driving you and Evie and Ellen in my truck," Irish said. "Case is following with your mom, Gwen and Mallory."

"And I'm staying with the boys," Molly said.

With the uncertainty of the weather coinciding with her actual due date—which the baby had completely ignored—they'd all moved into the Sutton house for the duration. It was a little cramped, but Evie knew Lane liked having everybody under one roof so nobody—especially one of their mothers—ended up trying to hurry on bad roads to get there in time.

"Are you having contractions, honey?" Laura asked, concern furrowing her brow.

"I don't really think so?"

"You'd know," Ellen, Laura and Mallory said at the same time.

"I'll get your bag," Mallory said. "Irish already packed extra cold-weather gear for everybody in his truck, just in case."

"Just in case of what?" Evie asked, but her sister was already gone.

The *what* became clear when they finally stepped out onto the porch and she heard the pinging sound of ice falling from the sky. Sleet was slightly better than freezing rain, but not by much.

"It snowed quite a bit first," Lane said, his arm around her waist. "There's a good base and we'll be fine."

"What if we get stuck? What if we slide off the road? How long would it take an ambulance to get to us?" Her mind was spinning out of control and she couldn't seem to rein it in. "What happens if I have to have this baby in the truck? None of us know how to do that, Lane."

"It can't be that different from pulling a calf," Irish said, and they all froze, staring at him. When he realized it, he gave Evie a sheepish smile. "Sorry. That was a joke."

Even though it was meant to be funny, Evie was oddly comforted by it. While she'd like to think her baby being born wouldn't be anything like pulling a calf, at least he'd assisted in a birth before.

Irish drove the truck right up to the house, jockeying it a few times so they just had to get Evie down the porch steps and right into the warm, spacious backseat.

Lane climbed in the back with her, while Ellen got in the front passenger seat, but Evie didn't like that. "Mom, you're going to spend the whole drive twisted around in your seat, and that's not safe and it'll distract Irish. There's enough room for you back here."

Once they were all buckled in and Case flashed his headlights to signal they were ready to follow, Irish pulled out onto the road and headed toward the hospital. It was a half hour on a good day and today was *not* a good day.

Evie tried not to think about what could go wrong. They weren't just taking two trucks so all the women could be there when the baby was born. She'd heard the guys talking and she knew the real reason was so if something happened to Irish's truck, they could move her to Case's and keep going. The whole thing was scary enough, but knowing her family had put so much thought into how to get her there safely was frightening, too.

Then the first real contraction hit and all she cared about was having Lane's hand to grip while her mother told her to breathe.

Luckily, Lane had been right in guessing the snow that had fallen first might help with traction. It took them an hour to make the half-hour drive to the hospital, but Evie didn't care. She hadn't given birth in a stuck truck on the side of the road. It was after hours, so Irish drove them right to the emergency room entrance, and she had a moment of panic when she didn't see headlights behind them.

"He's parking on the other side," Lane told her. "There's no parking here, but he followed us into the lot."

"Okay." She had a second to be thankful everybody had arrived in one piece—and to think to herself that in the future, one of the sisters should always stay home with the kids if the weather was bad—and then another contraction rolled over her. And this one was worse. "It's bad. I think the baby's coming *right now.*"

Nine hours later, Becca Leigh Thompson made her grand entrance and all Evie's fear and pain ceased to matter as they placed her baby girl on her chest. Lane bent over them, one hand on Evie's shoulder and the other covering her hands as she cradled the baby. She felt a tear drop from his cheek to hers and she looked up at him.

"Isn't she beautiful?" she whispered.

"She's as beautiful as her mother," he said, kissing her hair.

Then her mother kissed her cheek, running her hand over the baby's head. "She's gorgeous. I'm just going to go let everybody know, okay?"

Evie nodded, even though she would rather her mother stayed with her. But with the roads the way they were, Irish and Case had decided it made more sense for everybody to stay put in the waiting room, even though the hours had ticked by. It gave the plow trucks plenty of time to do their thing, and Molly didn't mind staying with the boys indefinitely.

"Let me know when everybody can come in, please," Ellen said to one of the nurses on her way out.

It was another hour before Evie was ready for a very short visit, and since she was the only mother in a double room, the nurse said they could all go in if they promised to behave.

More tears were shed, but they were the happiest of tears, and Evie soaked in all the love for her daughter. Becca was asleep on her chest, making the cutest sounds with her tiny mouth, and Lane had stretched himself out on the bed beside Evie, with his arm around her shoulders and one finger of his free hand clasped in his daughter's tiny fist.

"She's the most beautiful baby girl I've ever seen," Mallory said, and then she winked at Evie.

It was a stroke of luck that she had boys, so she could make that claim without playing favorites.

When the nurse finally stuck her head in and gave them a five-minute warning, Evie let them take pictures, even though she knew she probably looked like a train wreck.

Then Laura pulled a block of cream-colored knitting from her tote. "I grabbed a couple skeins and some needles, thinking I'd knit a few rows if we had to wait a little while. I've got almost half the blanket done."

They all laughed, and Evie shifted in her husband's arms, tipping her face up to his for a quick kiss.

"I love you," she whispered.

"I love you, too." Then he smiled so warmly she could almost feel it against her skin. "Both of you. My ladies."

Then came all the reluctant kisses goodbye from her family. They were all going to go, except Lane, of course. It had been a long night and they all needed proper food and some rest. But Irish promised to bring Ellen and Laura back tomorrow. And because the forecast for the next couple of days was unsettled, they'd already fit the base of Becca's car seat into Irish's truck, so he'd bring them home when it was time.

Then Gwen and Mallory were next to her and Mallory covered Evie's hand with hers. And then Gwen rested hers on top.

"I love you," Evie said, feeling the tears gather again.

"We love you, too," they said together, and then Mallory said, "I'm so glad you came home."

"Me, too," she said as Lane kissed her hair in silent agreement.

They were messy sometimes, this family of hers. But they loved each other fiercely, and there was nowhere else she'd rather be.

That storm was a doozy, folks! Remember to take it easy shoveling, and dig out those fire hydrants. If you parked your vehicle on the side of the street and now it's gone, Vinnie probably took it and you can reach out to the Stonefield PD to see how to get it back. The towing fee is on you and before you try to claim you didn't know about the winter parking ban, the warning's been published in every winter weekly edition of the Stonefield Gazette *since 1953, and we have the archives to prove it.*

In happier news, Evie Sutton and Lane Thompson welcomed their baby girl into the world during the storm! We here at the Gazette *thought it might be fun to name her in honor of the occasion, but Winter Storm Henry didn't give them a lot to work with. We'll let Evie and Lane share their baby girl's name, but Irish said there's already a glass with her name etched in it with the others on the shelf behind the bar, so if you really want to know, stop in and grab a pint.*

We'll see you at Sutton's Place Brewery & Tavern!

—Stonefield Gazette *Facebook Page*

* * * * *

WE HOPE YOU ENJOYED THIS BOOK FROM

⊕ HARLEQUIN

SPECIAL EDITION

Believe in love. Overcome obstacles. Find happiness.

Relate to finding comfort and strength in the support of loved ones and enjoy the journey no matter what life throws your way.

6 NEW BOOKS AVAILABLE EVERY MONTH!

Cierra's lips lifted in a smile that brightened his dark
corner of the coffee shop as she straightened. "Oh, good,
you remember me," she said, as if he could possibly
forget her.

How could he forget Cierra Greene? Head cheerleader,
class president, most popular girl in school and slayer of
teenage boys' hearts.

"Yeah...I remember you." He managed to keep his
voice calm even though his heart thumped as if he'd had
a dozen cappuccinos.

"I was worried because you didn't return any of my
calls." She tilted her head to the side and her thick, dark
hair shifted. Her smile didn't go away, but there was the
barest hint of accusation in her voice.

Wesley shifted in his seat. He hadn't returned her
calls because ever since the day Cierra told him after a

basketball game that she was ditching him for his former best friend, he'd vowed to never speak to her again. He realized vows made in high school didn't have to follow him into adulthood, but the moment he'd heard her voice message saying she'd like to meet up and talk, he'd deleted it and tried to move on with his life.

"I've been busy," he said.

"Good thing I caught you here, then, huh?" She moved to the opposite side of the table and pulled out the other chair and sat.

"How did you know I was here?"

"Mrs. Montgomery," she said, as if he should have known that one of the most respected women in town would give his whereabouts to her. She must have read the confusion on his face because she laughed, that lighthearted laugh that, unfortunately, still made his heart skip a beat. "When I couldn't reach you, my mom called around. Mrs. Montgomery said you typically spend Friday afternoons here. So, here I am!" She held out her arms and spoke as if she were a present.

Her bright smile and enthusiasm stunned him for a second. Wesley cleared his throat and took a sip of his coffee to compose himself. How many years later— fifteen—and he still had the lingering remnants of a crush on her?

Come on, Wes, you gotta do better than that!

He took a long breath and looked back at her. "Here you are."

Don't miss
The Spirit of Second Chances *by Synithia Williams,*
available September 2022 wherever
Harlequin Special Edition books and ebooks are sold.

Harlequin.com